How to Read This Book

Enjoying this book is really pretty easy—this isn't rocket science. It's all about love, and in love we're all allowed to take a turn.

Start reading at the beginning like you would any novel, but when you reach a crossroads and are presented with a few questions, look deep into your heart to discover the true path you should take. Then turn to the page indicated and continue reading the story from there.

Don't read straight through, because it all will seem terribly muddled that way.

Of course you will be tempted to go back to the previous choice when you reach a displeasing outcome. Go ahead— everyone does this, and it is quite wonderful to be able to retrace your steps. If only real life afforded us that option! Keeping a bookmark—or a finger—between the pages at the most recent turning point is recommended for efficiency.

Are you ready to take your first steps toward finding true love?

Good.

Now go and follow your heart.

—J. E. Bright

FOLLOW YOUR HEART

Your Best Friend's Boyfriend

J. E. BRIGHT

SCHOLASTIC INC.

New York   Toronto   London   Auckland   Sydney

Mexico City   New Delhi   Hong Kong   Buenos Aires

ISBN 0-439-79140-5

Book design by Steve Scott

12 11 10 9 8 7 6 5 4 3 2 1   6 7 8 9 10 11/0

Printed in the U.S.A.   40

First printing, January 2006

To my best friend, David, for having different taste,
and for making me laugh.

Your best friend, Sally, lets out a long, happy sigh. "Isn't Mike gorgeous?" she asks you. "Check out those cute legs!"

From your seat next to her in the second row of the bleachers, you scan the soccer field. The guys on your high school's team, the Clearview Stallions, are wearing dark green jerseys and matching shorts, and their opponents, the North Cliff Eagles, are wearing blue uniforms. You shade your eyes from the sun with your hand. "Which one's Mike?" you ask. All the North Cliff guys look pretty much alike from where you're sitting. All of them have cute legs.

Sally points a perfectly manicured finger toward the far end of the field. "There," she says. "With the black hair. Facing off against your brother."

As a photographer for your school newspaper, you always have your digital camera with you. You peer through the viewfinder and zoom in on the guy she pointed out. Mike crouches in ready position on defense as your brother Peter hurtles toward him, dribbling the ball at top speed. You smile as you see Peter touch his lucky headband in a habitual gesture as he closes in on Mike.

Mike has a trim, athletic body with a golden tan and a look of intense determination on his handsome face. The lean

1

muscles in his arms and legs clench as he concentrates. His sweaty hair glistens in the sunlight. You take his picture, feeling self-conscious about your suddenly thumping heart.

"He's adorable," you tell Sally without lowering the camera. You mean it, too, which is strange, since you and she usually have totally different tastes in guys.

"Today's our one week anniversary," Sally says proudly. "We're going to a movie tonight —" She gasps as your brother fakes out Mike on the field. Mike lurches the wrong way and Peter sweeps around him.

You click the camera again, capturing Mike tumbling to his knees and hitting the ground hard. A second later, Peter takes a shot on goal and scores for the Stallions.

"Your brother's the only one who can fake Mike out," Sally says, sounding slightly defensive. She pushes her shoulder-length, straight red hair back behind her ears. "He's usually incredible, I swear."

"I can tell," you say, wondering how Sally would feel if the photo of Mike falling showed up in your school newspaper.

After the game, which the Stallions win three to two, you follow Sally down to the field. Mike is sitting on the visitors' bench, looking dejected as he takes off his cleats.

Sally sits down next to Mike and bumps his shoulder with her own. "Don't worry about the game," she coos. "You were wonderful!"

Mike shrugs. "We blew it," he says. "But we'll get you guys next time."

Sally peers up at you. The skin on her pale face is always somewhat pink, but now her cheeks are turning bright red simply from her excitement at being near her boyfriend. "Mike," she says, "I want you to meet my best friend. She's the sister of Peter, the guy who . . . well, the guy who scored in the first half."

Mike shifts around on the bench and nods at you. "Yeah," he says. "You do look like brother and sister."

You swallow as you nod back at Mike. His eyes are the most mesmerizing electric blue you've ever seen. You look down at your camera quickly and click the camera shutter open and closed again for no good reason.

There's an awkward pause as you try to think of something to say.

It surprises you to realize how much you want to impress him.

If you tell Mike about the photograph you took, turn to page 7. ➡️

If you praise Mike for his performance in the game, turn to page 57. ➡️

If you cut the tension by making a joke about your brother, turn to page 109. ➡️

3

♥ "Mike?" you say with a laugh. "He totally means nothing to me."

Sally folds her arms across her chest. "Then why do you keep looking back to see if he's still there?"

"I'm just curious!" you protest. "It's funny — he's been following us around."

Sally walks over to a bench beside a small fountain and sits down. You follow, but you don't sit — instead you stand in front of her.

"You're lying," she says. "I know when you're lying."

"I'm totally not!" you argue, but you can feel your face flushing. She's not wrong — you do feel something for Mike, and you've been nurturing a lump of desire for him since the moment you met him, but there's no way you can say that to Sally. "Really, Sal," you say. "I couldn't care less about him."

Sally sighs. Her face crumples, and you worry for a second that she might start crying. "It's doesn't matter, I guess," she says. "He's not into me, anyway."

"Yes, he is," you tell her, although you hope he's not. It feels awfully disloyal, but you can't help hoping that Mike dumps her soon and asks you out instead.

Without looking at you, Sally stands up, her arms hanging limply at her sides. "I think I'm going home now," she says. "Why don't you call me later, okay?

"Okay," you say, and you stand awkwardly in the middle of the mall as you watch her shuffle away, wiping her eyes.

You sit down in the spot on the bench where Sally had been, feeling just awful. Sally knew you were lying, and you knew she knew, but somehow your friendship just wasn't strong enough to break through those lies and become real again.

Swallowing deeply, you fight back tears of your own.

You failed a loyalty test, and you don't like yourself very much at this moment at all.

But maybe if something happens with Mike, it will all be worth it . . . ?

Nothing happens with Mike. Sally goes out with him for another week before they break up, but she doesn't even talk to you about it. She doesn't answer her phone when you call, and eventually you get tired of leaving voice mails, text messages, and IMs that she never returns.

Two months later you and she barely acknowledge each other in the hallway.

The next time you see Mike, he's in front of a coffee shop, making out with some tall, beautiful girl with long brown hair. He glances up when you walk by, and you give him a little wave, but he just looks at you blankly and then goes back to kissing the leggy brunette.

Which is okay, because you've got a big crush on a guy named Hugo by that point.

But nobody you meet will ever make up for the loss of your best friend.

The End.

"Hey," you blurt out, holding up your camera to show Mike. "I kind of caught a moment during the game. It's a great shot, and you're in it —"

Mike's eyebrows go up in a cute, interested expression. "Oh, yeah? Cool."

"See?" Sally says. "I've got media connections."

You take a deep breath, unsure how Mike will react to the truth about the photo. "But the pic doesn't show you in the best light," you tell Mike. "I mean, actually the *lighting* is great, but you might not be flattered by how I caught you. You're falling."

"Delete it," says Sally. "Easy as pie to say goodbye."

"No!" both you and Mike reply at the same time. "It's —"

Mike laughs.

You hug your camera to your chest, protecting it. "You first," you tell Mike.

Looking down, Mike pulls a shin guard out of his long soccer sock. "Honesty is important in art, isn't it? Don't delete it — unless you want to. I can handle the truth."

While Mike's head is down, you take the opportunity to sneak a peek at his legs close up. He has big calf muscles. His bent kneecaps are round and cute. You glance up at

7

Sally, and she's looking at Mike's legs, too. Your eyes meet and Sally smiles. "Hot," she mouths at you.

You can only manage a weak smile as you nod in agreement.

While Mike packs his gym bag, you feel a sudden rush of courage. "Stop by our newspaper office," you say, "and I'll print you out a copy of the photo. I caught some other good ones today, too."

"I'd like to see them," Mike replies. He puts his arm around Sally, and you try to ignore the need to cringe. Sally is your best friend! You two have shared secrets since third grade — who else would have kept the raspberry jam incident a secret? You should be happy that she found Mike.

Sally rests her head on Mike's shoulder. "Or you could just give the printouts to me," she says. "I'll see Mike again before you will."

"That would work, too," you say.

Mike stands up and hoists his bag over his shoulder. "You ready?" he asks Sally.

"Mike's driving me home so I can get ready for our date tonight," she tells you. "Want him to drop you off on the way?"

"It's no problem," Mike says. He looks right at you and you don't know how to interpret his expression — it's intense and direct. Does he want you to come with them?

You know you shouldn't. It's not good, this feeling that you want to stay in Mike's company. It's bad. Sally's friendship is too important to you. "No, thanks," you say. "I'm going back to the newspaper office to get some stuff done."

Mike nods, and heads toward the parking lot. Sally lingers beside you for a moment until he's out of earshot. "You were great," she says. "He's cute, right?"

"Very," you agree, trying to sound casual. "He's into you, I can tell. Hold on to this one."

She giggles. "Yeah, I will," she replies. "OK, got to run." Sally gives you a quick hug and then hurries after Mike.

He's opening his car door when he sees you looking, and he waves. You wave back. Mike's car is a beat-up old BMW. It's the color of champagne.

"Enjoy the movie!" you shout, and then you stand there and watch as they drive out of the parking lot.

With a big sigh, you turn toward your school. Your brother Peter is coming out of the side door with a couple of the Stallions. "Good job, guys," you tell them as you pass by. "I got some good shots for the paper."

"All in a day's work," Peter replies. "And now we are off to celebrate the total and utter destruction of the North Cliff Eagles." Which gets a bunch of hand-slapping from his teammates. You know the other guys — Dave and Carlos. Both of them are pretty cute. Carlos, in particular, has a sweet, sexy smile. He's also in your English class, and he usually has intelligent things to say about the books your class is reading.

"Winning by one goal is not utter destruction," you tease, and then you start to push past them into the school.

If you continue on your way to the newspaper office, turn to Page 13. ➡

If you stop to flirt with Carlos, turn to page 22. ➡

This whole midnight serenading bit is just too wacky for you to handle. Mike is obviously obsessed with you in an unhealthy way, and you honestly can say that you're afraid of him. Yeah, he's just singing to you, but you know that if you tell him to go away, it will only get worse. How long will it be before he's waiting to catch you alone in some dark place, or he's lurking in the bushes in front of your house, waiting for you to come outside when you least suspect he's around?

The dispatcher at 911 is very understanding, and she sounds kind, which helps you calm down. It doesn't take long for a police cruiser to pull up in front of your house.

As you watch from your window, a cop gets out and talks to Mike, and he looks up at your window once before he heads over to his own car and drives away.

Once he's gone, you meet the policewoman at your front door. Your parents and Peter are awake now, and all of you gather around the kitchen table for tea while the cop explains your options.

Your parents help you decide to get a restraining order placed on Mike. He's not allowed to come within fifty feet of you at any time, and he's not allowed near your house.

It was a good thing you got the restraining order, because

a week later, the cops find Mike hiding in a tree in your front yard, trying to peep into your bedroom window.

Luckily, you were downstairs at the time, watching TV with Sally.

After they take Mike away, you never see him again.

And good riddance.

The End.

The Clear View newspaper office is empty — this week's issue was just put to bed yesterday. You get to work, uploading the photos, adjusting contrast and brightness, and cropping the shots to make them more dynamic. You leave the pictures of Mike for last.

When you finally do open the first one, you let out a long, slow breath. You can be a harsh critic sometimes about your own work, but you know this is a really good photo. Mike is crouched in ready position on the field, his face set with concentration. His features shine in the sunlight with the shadow of his cheekbone standing out in sharp contrast, making the picture totally dramatic.

You zoom in closer on Mike, blowing up his image so you can see every pore on his face. He has a tiny zit on his chin, and this blemish on his otherwise flawless skin makes you like him even more. You're glad to know he's not perfect.

The door opens, and Mike sticks his head in. You click the photo file closed quickly, hoping your sudden blush isn't obvious.

"Uh . . . hi," Mike says. "Good, I found you. I dropped off Sally, and then I had to pass by your school on my way home anyway, so . . ." He trails off and glances down the hallway before turning to face you again. "I wanted to see the photo you took."

You pull up the second photo on screen. "Sure," you say. Mike comes over to the computer station and peers over your shoulder. You're hyperaware of how close he is to you. It makes you feel slightly lightheaded.

In the picture, Mike's on his knees in the grass, and you can tell by little flecks of dirt flying into the air just how hard he hit. His hands are clenched into fists, his hair is wild, and his eyes burn with pure intensity.

Mike stays quiet a moment.

You start getting nervous. "I can still delete it if you want me to —"

"No," Mike says softly. "It's just . . . powerful. Like, that's sports, right there in that picture. You win some and you lose some, but you can tell that even though I crashed, I'm not giving up. You know I'm getting back in the game."

"Yeah," you reply. Your heart starts thumping again as he leans in for a closer look. He's so close now you can smell his sweat from the game. It's not gross at all, and you close your eyes for a second, memorizing the scent. "Exactly. That's exactly what I thought, too."

"It's a great picture," he says. "Really good . . . composition. Will you e-mail it to me?"

"Of course, yes," you say. "I'll do it now so I don't forget. Hey . . . what would you think if we ran this picture in our school newspaper?" You'll probably run it even if he doesn't want you to, but you'd feel a lot better if he didn't mind.

Mike stands up straight and smooths down his blue jersey, thinking about it. "Go for it," he says finally. "I mean, it is a little embarrassing because we lost, but I'm not going to stand in the way of the truth."

"You sound pretty smart for a soccer jock," you tease him. You're actually pleasantly surprised that he seems intelligent at all — Sally doesn't usually go for the brainy ones. He's even insightful, talking about truth in art.

Mike laughs. "Thanks," he says. "My life isn't all about soccer. I'm into a lot of other stuff, too."

"Like Sally?" you ask.

"Yeah," he says, "but even besides her, I'm crazy busy. You really want to know?"

"Sure, tell me," you reply.

"OK. I'm learning to play the guitar and taking lessons on Saturdays at that guitar shop on Montgomery Avenue."

"I know the place," you say. "My parents' dry cleaner is right there."

"But my favorite thing right now is an internship I got at a veterinarian's office," Mike continues. "I'm probably going to be a vet someday."

"That's awesome," you say. "Really. I love animals, too. I've got two cats and a dog at home."

"Actually, I need to stop by the vet's office to walk the

dogs sometime tonight before . . . before my date," says Mike. He licks his lips and glances toward the door. "It's really cool hanging out in that office, with all the animals. The dogs are always so psyched to see me. I was kind of thinking I'd head over there now. . . ."

You're confused. Was that an implied invitation to go with him . . . or was Mike making an excuse to take off? If he's inviting you, you'd love to go, but you had plans to work on your own project for the citywide student art show in a few days. Also, how disloyal to Sally would it be for you to hang out with her newest boyfriend? You can't help wondering how upset she would be if she knew. Maybe you should brush him off gently. . . . The important thing here is staying true to your best friend.

Or maybe you should break through the uncertainty and accept his offer. Sally would probably be thrilled that her best friend and her boyfriend are getting along.

If you nonchalantly tell Mike, "Okay, see you around," turn to page 213. ➡️

If you tell Mike that you would love to see the vet's office, turn to page 167. ➡️

"How do I feel about Mike?" you say to Sally. "I don't feel much of anything, really. He seems like a decent, cute guy overall, but that's it, you know? He doesn't really do it for me. I don't think I would even notice him in a crowd."

It takes a few minutes to convince Sally that you're sincere, but after you give her the secret swear that only the two of you know, she finally gets that you're being honest.

"Should I keep seeing him?" she asks. "Tell me what you really think, truly."

You glance across the mall again, but Mike has vanished. "I don't know," you reply. "I don't think I can answer that for you."

"Come on," Sally pleads. "It's your job as my best friend to give me your honest opinion. I'd do it for you!"

"I know you would," you say with a sigh. "Okay, no. Honestly, really honestly, I think he's creepy. He was totally staring at me and ignoring you in front of the music store, and that's just not right. Yeah, he's great-looking, but come on — you can do so much better, Sal. You don't need to be hanging around a guy who stalks your best friend when he should be worshipping the ground you walk on. Besides, he's pretty dumb."

Sally closes her eyes and nods. "Yeah," she says. "I think I knew that. I just needed to hear it from someone I trust." She looks at you and smiles sadly. "Thank you so much for telling me the truth."

"Anytime," you tell Sally, and you hug her tightly.

After another hour or so of shopping, you and Sally split up, walking home in different directions.

The walk is fine . . . until you have to cut along the back edge of a warehouse to cross the railroad tracks that are between the shopping area and your neighborhood. It's in an overgrown, bushy section of the path, the only light is from a distant streetlamp, and there's nobody else around. You've walked this route dozens of times, but your heart always beats faster here.

A guy comes around the corner of the warehouse a few feet in front of you. You stop short, peering at him in the murky darkness.

"I heard what you said about me," the guy says.

It's Mike. But why does his voice sound so different . . . so unhinged . . . so *scary*?

"What I said?" you repeat. "What did I say?"

He glares at you, and the expression on his face makes you really nervous — his eyes are dark and blank, but he's grinding his teeth together with a horrible crunching sound. "You told Sally that you don't love me," he hisses at you. "You told her that I'm creepy and that she shouldn't see me anymore."

18

You laugh, sounding a lot more nervous than you intended. "Creepy?" you ask. "I can't imagine why I called you creepy — and here you are lurking behind a warehouse in the dark, waiting for me."

Mike steps toward you, and you step backward.

"I love you, you know," he says. "From the first second Sally introduced us, I loved you like a sun was exploding in my heart. Like there was a nuclear bomb in my brain. Like a volcano erupting."

"Okay," you say, and you turn to run.

Mike sticks his foot out, catching your ankle, and you trip, falling heavily to your knees.

You glance up at him and see that he's pulled out a black kerchief, which he snaps in the air once, before winding it around his hands to make a garrote. To choke you.

Stupid boy.

Maybe you should have told him that you've been taking karate since you were twelve years old.

You learned all about disarming an assailant *ages* ago.

Calmly, you climb to your feet and face Mike, staring right into his blue eyes, now swirling with scary wildness that convinces you he's completely crazy.

You lower yourself quickly into a squat. Then you crouch forward, scuttling toward him. He looks surprised, and you take advantage of his uncertainty by scooping up a handful of dusty gravel from the path and hurling it into his eyes.

You launch up, smacking him with both fists right in the stomach. He tries to catch your neck with the outstretched kerchief, but you block him by knocking his wrist off course with the heaviest part of your forearm. He loses his balance, and you help him fall by giving him an extra shove. He lands in a pile of old newspapers tangled in some weeds, and a rat zips over his head, squealing.

You run back toward the mall.

The first shop you reach is a Quik-Stop convenience store. You run inside and rush up to the counter, where a woman has her mouth open, staring at you in mid-chew. You can see a big wad of purple bubblegum in her mouth.

"Call the police!" you tell the woman.

She starts chewing her gum again. "Why, honey?"

Through the store window, you can see Mike hurtling into the parking lot and stopping to look around. He spots you and starts striding toward the store.

"He attacked me," you tell the woman. "And here he comes."

"Uh-uh," the woman says. "He's not getting in here." She reaches under the counter and presses a button, and the entry door locks. "That button summons the police, too, honey," she tells you.

Mike runs up to the window and screams something at you — you can barely hear him — and bangs on the glass with his fists. You jump nervously.

"He won't hurt you," the clerk tells you. "I've been in this situation before. He can't get in, I promise. Want some gum?"

"Sure," you reply.

Mike stops banging when sirens start screeching somewhere behind him.

You spot glowing red and blue lights coming around the corner, and you let yourself relax.

After kicking the window twice, Mike tries to run.

He doesn't get far before the police cruisers cut him off.

Attempted high school homicide is not a crime the authorities take lightly.

The place Mike's going, you doubt there will be a soccer team.

Or any girls for him to stalk.

The End.

♥ "Carlos," you say, stopping in front of him, "can I talk to you for a second?"

"Uh . . . sure," he says. "Hey, you guys — I'll catch up." Your brother and Dave just shake their heads and keep walking. Carlos smiles down at you — he's really tall, probably something like six foot three. "So, what's up?"

"You were great out there today," you say. "I saw that goal you headed in. That was an awesome play." You accidentally brush your hand down the side of Carlos's muscular arm, and you smile when he shivers. He's very handsome — beefier than Sally's boyfriend, with a sweet, trusting face.

"Oh, thanks," he says, shifting nervously. "It helped that you were in the stands, cheering us on."

"Yeah?" you say. "I didn't know you noticed I was there."

"I always notice when you're there —" Carlos begins, but then he realizes he's admitted too much, and he cuts himself off.

"I always notice you, too," you tell him.

"It's nice to have someone so pretty cheering for me," Carlos says.

You giggle. "Stop," you say. "You're embarrassing me."

"Good," Carlos replies with a smile. "Hey, you want to come with us to celebrate?"

You return his smile, which is open and genuine. "I can't right now," you say apologetically. "I've got some stuff I need to catch up on. But listen, next game, when you see me waving my hands in the air, know that's just for you, okay?"

"Okay," Carlos says, still grinning. "Cool."

On your way into the newspaper office, you realize that yeah, Sally's boyfriend is cute, but you need a guy who makes you feel special, a guy with whom you feel a real connection. Sally can keep Mike. Who needs him when you have guys like Carlos to flirt with?

And if Carlos doesn't work out, there's always his friend Dave . . . or that guy Steven in your math class. . . .

Suddenly the possibilities seem endless.

The End.

♥ You bite your bottom lip, deeply moved by Mike's declaration of love. You had barely allowed yourself to hope that someone so popular and handsome would ever be interested in you, but now it seems like your secret dream is coming true.

"Okay, okay," you call to him. "I'll be right down."

You pull on your new pink robe and make a stop in the bathroom to wash your face (and apply just a touch of concealer) before you go downstairs and open the front door. It's dark outside except for a lamppost illuminating the street and a small sconce lantern above your front stoop.

Mike is waiting for you at the bottom of the stairs with a tulip in his hands, which looks black in the darkness. He holds it out to you.

"Is that one of my mother's tulips?" you ask.

"Uh —" Mike says.

"Never mind," you tell him. "I'll tell her the neighbor's dog killed another one of her flowers. She's already crazy mad at that dog anyway." You take the flower from Mike — it's actually orange, you can now tell in the lantern light. "Thanks," you say, rewarding him with a dazzling smile.

He blinks and swallows.

24

You sit down on the front stoop and pat the space on the slate tile next to you. "Have a seat," you say.

Mike sits.

A few minutes ago he was singing to you and making declarations of love . . . but now he doesn't seem to know what to say. You will not let an uncomfortable silence happen between you. Not now.

"So . . . ," you begin. "What brought this on? You coming over and serenading me?"

"Oh," Mike says, "I don't know." He ducks his head, then tilts it to look over at you. "I was lying in bed, and I just kept imagining talking to you over and over again, and I just couldn't fall asleep. I wanted to talk to you, to get to know you, to make sure . . . to be sure that what I'm feeling isn't all made up in my head."

"It's not," you say. "This is reality. You're here, talking to me."

Mike smiles at you, a tender grin that makes your toes curl with delight. "I'm glad," he says. "I'm glad I came over and made this happen. I'm so glad you came downstairs. I'm glad this is *happening*, you know?"

"I know," you say.

Your conversation with Mike that night starts out slow, with just halting discussions of what classes you're taking and the things you're interested in (Mike: soccer, math, and politics; you: history, flute, historical novels, and chocolate). By the time your talk has moved on to TV, movies, and music, you already feel incredibly comfortable around him, and you feel like you have so much to tell him that you know he will just understand instantly. He isn't dumb at all . . . just shy with his opinions, and careful about how much he reveals. It's amazing how many pop culture things you two share. He gets your TV references, and he thinks the same movies are so funny.

After a few hours of talking to Mike, you almost forget that you barely knew him before yesterday — it feels like you've climbed into each other's brains and are sitting inside each other's personalities, looking around and approving of what you see.

The conversation shifts into really personal territory — Mike's parents' divorce, your grandfather dying last year, your hopes for college and the cities you want to live in — and before you know it, the first fingers of dawn are reaching out over the houses across the street, turning the sky a beautiful pale blue that matches the magic of Mike's eyes.

"Have you ever had a real boyfriend?" Mike asks you.

You think about telling him about John, this guy you had a deep crush on a few months ago, but now that you're sitting with Mike and feeling all these new feelings about him, you can barely remember what John looks like. "Not really," you say. "Nobody important."

"Do you want one?" Mike asks. He bites the edge of his index finger, and you suddenly get how scary that question was for him to ask.

26

"Yes," you reply. "If the right guy asked me to go out with him, I'd be ready for that."

"Like if I asked you to be my girlfriend, you'd say yes?"

"Try me."

Mike blushes deeply and looks at you very seriously. "Will you?" he asks. "Be my girlfriend? Say yes."

"Totally," you say. "One hundred percent yes."

Mike's smile grows so big that it must hurt his cheeks . . . the same way yours are hurting. He's so happy that his head is bobbing strangely. Then he looks deep into your eyes with his breathtaking blue gaze and slowly leans toward you.

The sprinklers in your front yard suddenly spring to life, hissing and clicking. You and Mike both laugh and pull your feet up onto the second step so they won't get wet. The sun's rays are now hitting the spraying sprinkler water, casting tiny rainbows in flying fragments above the grass.

"Oh," you say, and you grab Mike's face between your hands and pull him toward you for a long, lingering kiss that feels more intense and amazing than you ever imagined in your hottest dreams.

"Is this love?" Mike asks, his forehead against yours, his long, dark eyelashes tickling the bridge of your nose. "It feels like love."

"It's love," you answer blissfully. "It's love."

The End.

Mike downs a swig of the nasty mixture . . . but at the last minute, you don't. He gags once, but then manages to guzzle the whole cupful.

"I lose," you say flatly. "Oh, well."

The other guys laugh at this, but then they cut off all sound when Mike's shoulders heave up once, and he leans over and grips the front of the sink. His knuckles turn bright red, then white.

Sally puts her hand on his back. "Are you okay?"

"Don't touch me!" Mike snaps.

Sally snatches her hand back like he was too hot. *"Fine,"* she replies, stung.

His body heaves again. "Ohhhh," he moans. "Nooooo."

Mike's whole body shudders. A cough comes from too deep in his chest, and he tries to cut it off.

He gags again, and you can tell he just threw up in his mouth a little.

You are very sure the taste of Sally's potion did not improve on the way back up.

"It looks like Sally's going to win . . ." says Jazz.

Sally laughs. "Be a man and hold your hurl!" she tells Mike. "Don't think about the taste in your mouth. . . . Does it taste like fried eggs and clams . . . on a barbecue?"

Mike hacks for a second, then stands up straight and glares at all of you, his handsome face a sickly pea green. He gags once more before bolting from the room.

The other guys — and Sally — howl with laughter.

You manage a weak smile. It's kind of funny, but you feel sorry for Mike.

"The winner!" Walt exclaims, raising Sally's arm in the air like a champion. It doesn't escape your notice that he's now holding Sally's hand.

"Nice," you snark at Sally.

She just shrugs, and brings her arm down . . . and then finally drops Walt's fingers.

You turn and chase after Mike.

He's only a little way down the hall, leaning against the wall, curled over a bit, with his palm pressed against his mouth.

You grab his arm. "C'mon," you order him, and you propel him down the hall toward the bathroom, pushing past two girls to get there.

The door's locked. You knock on it. "Emergency!" you shout.

"Just a minute!" a girl calls sweetly from inside.

Mike is having dry heaves next to you.

"Ew," one girl says.

"I know," says the other, and they both hurry away.

Upstairs, you think. There have got to be more bathrooms upstairs. You glance at Mike. He's taking jagged deep breaths, but still fighting the don't-barf battle of his life . . . and losing.

You give him a push from behind. "Go!" you tell him. "Upstairs! *Now!*"

Mike shakes his head, refusing, but you give him another shove and he starts climbing the stairs, moaning the whole way up. You honestly don't think he's going to make it, and you can just picture how hard it is going to be to get vomit off the pale yellow carpet covering the stairs.

There's a dainty half bath just off to the side of the landing. Mike pushes inside, making a beeline for the bowl.

He drops to his knees on a fuzzy, dark blue mat, and ralphs up a bucketful of sick. There's spaghetti and carrot in it, which is indescribably nasty, but worst of all is the sound of the barf hitting the water.

If you take pity on Mike and rub his back while he's hurling, turn to page 205. ➡️

If you decide this whole barfing deal is just too nasty and you're out of there pronto, turn to page 179. ➡️

♥ "Let's sit down," you say. "I want to be sitting down when we talk about this. And I need something to drink — you want a smoothie?"

"Yogurt, bananas, and peaches," Sally replies. She goes to secure a table in the food court, and you head over to the smoothie stand.

While you're waiting for your drinks to frappé in the blender, you realize that you should just come clean to Sally about the feelings you've been having about Mike. Yes, you're attracted to him. Maybe a lot. You're not going to be able to hide that from Sally for much longer, and it just kills you to even think of lying to her. If you just tell her how you feel, perhaps she'll be upset, but it will be good to get this problem out on the table where you both can deal with it, just like the two of you have always dealt with issues together.

As you carry the smoothies over to Sally, you realize that, despite your resolve to tell her the truth, the idea of actually saying it is making you quite nervous. Your hand shakes a little when you place Sally's drink down in front of her and pass her a straw.

"Okay," Sally says after you've sat down and situated

yourself. She sounds as nervous as you feel. "You were going to tell me exactly what kind of feelings you have for Mike."

"Yes," you say, nodding slowly. "I have . . . strong feelings for him. I'm not sure what those feelings *are*, exactly . . . but they're strong."

Sally's face turns red, and she takes a long, thoughtful sip of her smoothie.

"Not that I would ever act on it!" you assure her quickly. "He's *your* boyfriend, I know that, and I would never get between the two of you. Never. I can control myself. If you want, we can totally forget this conversation ever happened and you'll never notice that I feel anything for Mike —"

"I'm over him," Sally blurts out. "I'm *so* over him. We're through."

You sit back in the uncomfortable food court chair and remain silent for a moment, absorbing this. "When did this . . . ," you begin, but then trail off. "Um, why?"

"I'm not stupid," Sally replies. "I can see how he looks at you. It wasn't me he was following around the mall today. You know me — I need a guy who worships me and isn't always craning his neck around to stare at other girls. Especially not my best friend."

You take a long sip of your blueberry smoothie. "If you want, I won't pay any attention to him," you offer loyally. "He can just cease to exist for us both."

"Thanks," Sally says. "Do you want to . . . pay attention to him?"

"Only if it doesn't bother you," you reply.

Sally smiles. "It doesn't bother me," she says. "If you want him, go for it. I know he likes you."

"You're sure?" you ask. You mean both that it's okay with her and that he likes you.

"I'm sure," Sally replies.

That night, you lie in bed trying to fall asleep, but the pillow won't stop bunching up uncomfortably, your legs feel too hot under the blankets and too cold outside the covers, and your brain won't shut up about Mike. Now that Sally's given you permission to go after him, you can't stop thinking of a million things you want to say to him, none of which sound right when you imagine saying them out loud.

A sudden sharp sound at your second-floor window startles you, and you stiffen, your face flushing and your heart racing with automatic night terror.

After a pause, the sound happens again — a quick rap against the glass. This second time, it's obvious that someone is tossing pebbles at your window.

You slide out of bed and crawl the few feet to the window, hiding under it so you can't be seen from outside. Then you peek around the curtains down at the lawn.

It's Mike. He bends over and picks up another pebble and gets ready to throw it.

You pull open the window and stick your head out. "Stop!" you call down to him in a loud whisper. "I'm here. Hi." It's a good thing your parents' bedroom window is on the other side of the house . . . and that Peter can sleep through anything.

"Hi," Mike says. "Can you come down?"

You think about that for a moment — you're wearing your rattiest T-shirt and sweatpants as pajamas, but you could throw on your new light robe. On the other hand, you rubbed a new salicylic acid skin cream all over your face before you went to bed, and that's probably a chalky mess close up. "That's not a good idea," you reply. "Not right now."

"Oh, okay," Mike says. He sounds really disappointed. "I just wanted to see you, that's all."

He starts to walk away across the lawn, but after a few steps — before you've even had a chance to retreat — he turns around and hurries back under your window.

Then he begins to sing.

You recognize the song immediately — it's crazy popular and is up for consideration as your school's prom theme song this year. You cringe. How embarrassing is *this*?

After a second of listening to him, though, you relax a little. He's not bad, and he's singing softly enough that it doesn't sound too horribly obnoxious.

Mike cuts off his song. "I can't help it," he tells you. "I'm falling for you. You're all I can think about. Can't you please come down and just talk to me?"

34

If you think he's kind of charming and you go down to talk to him, turn to page 24. ➤

If you think he's crossed a line into derangement and you call the cops on him, turn to Page 11. ➤

♥ After considering what to do for a second, you step forward to kiss Mike. But he takes a step backward at the same time, catching you off balance.

You fall to the side and grab the edge of the developer bath, sloshing the liquid onto your shoes. Mike catches you under your arms and stops you from falling to the floor.

"Oops," you say, and let out a really stupid-sounding giggle that you cut off immediately. "I guess I tripped."

"Sorry, are you all right?" he asks.

"Fine, fine," you reply, pulling away from him and shaking the developer off your foot. The liquid glows on your shoe in the red safelight. You're not hurt — just horribly embarrassed.

"I'm really sorry," Mike says. "If you're sure you're okay, I've got to go. I've got to stop at the vet's and walk the dogs now, or I'll be late for the movie with Sally."

"I'm good," you say. "See you around. Say hi for me and have fun."

He meets your eyes and holds your gaze for a long, lingering moment before he turns and pushes through the blackout curtain, leaving the darkroom.

When he's gone, you slump down onto a stool and hold

your head in your hands. Your cheeks feel hot and flushed. Memories of things Mike said — *You have the talent to capture it in art* — and when you said Sally is beautiful — *So are you* — sear your mind, making you feel even warmer.

You take a deep breath. Oh, that awful almost-kiss — you can't believe you actually fell over. You hope Mike didn't realize what you were going for. You cringe, trying to forget.

And then he ran off for his date with Sally.

That's for the best, anyway, right? Sally is your best friend — and you couldn't ask for a better one. Who else would have helped you throw that funeral for Twinkles, your guinea pig, and done it so solemnly and meaningfully, both of you crying together as you buried him in the backyard?

It was really bad that you tried to kiss Mike. Yes, he's adorable, and yes, it felt really natural getting so close to him, but you let yourself get carried away. You will not do that again. Ever!

Oh, but the way his lips looked in the red light, so lush and soft. It's like you were hypnotized by his lips.

What really got to you, though, even more than how cute he is, was the way he talked about your photography. He was interested, he wanted to learn what you knew. There's so much more you want to know about him, too, like his favorite songs to play on his guitar, or why he's so into animals, or why, exactly, he's thinks you're beautiful.

As you get back to printing out your photos, Sally's trusting, happy face in the next shot makes you feel just awful.

"I'm sorry," you tell Sally's photo. "It won't happen again."

Turn to page 46. ➡

♥ Yawn. In your book, sports talk even beats out computer talk or video game talk or car talk as the most boring kind of guy conversation in the universe. You have no problem with playing sports — you're actually quite good at basketball and volleyball — but you just can't understand why guys hash out the same athletic events over and over again, spouting statistics and records at each other. The way they repeat the same things, it's almost as if they're talking about sports as a code for something else entirely.

"Let's get out of here," you whisper to Sally. "Let's go shopping."

Sally nods. "Let me just finish my salad," she replies.

"Hurry," you say. You push the remnants of your fries away from you, and drain the last of your soda. "Okay, North Cliff studs," you tell the guys, "this has been fascinating, but we've got things to do."

"See ya," Walt says. So much for any romantic interest in him — there's no spark at all between you and Walt. There's something about his skin that makes him look like he's made out of rubbery plastic, anyway.

"Where are you going?" Mike asks, just as Sally shoves the last forkful of her salad into her mouth.

"We've got important girl business to attend to," you reply. "In the mall."

"Girls and malls," he teases you.

"Boys and sports," you shoot back.

Mike laughs. "At least sports is good for something," he says. "It's useful, keeping healthy."

"Shopping can be a workout, too," Sally adds earnestly. "I've felt totally exhausted after a long day hitting the stores."

"Plus," you say, "shopping actually helps prepare you for the future, while sports does nothing."

"Yeah?" Packer asks. "How so?"

You stand up and throw some money for your food down on the table. "How often are you going to play soccer when you're fifty?" you reply. "But you're going to shop until you die."

Mike laughs again, obviously appreciating what you're saying. "So go," he tells you. "Go prepare for your future."

Sally gives Mike's arm a little squeeze before she slides out of the booth. You find it odd that she doesn't kiss him goodbye, or even look back at him as you and she leave the diner.

The north entrance to the mall is only a short walk across the parking lot. "Anything in particular you need?" you ask Sally as you open the doors and step into the cold mall air.

"A new belt," Sally replies. "I need one with some color to it. All of mine are so drab."

"So that means new shoes to match, too, of course."

"Of course," Sally says with a giggle.

An hour or so later, you're perusing the new releases in the music store when you catch a glimpse of a blue North Cliff jersey pulling back abruptly from the store window. You hold up a CD, pretending not to be paying any attention, but watching the window in the case's reflection. After another few seconds, you see a flash of the blue jersey again. You could swear you recognized Mike's handsome features before he disappeared again.

You calmly walk over to where Sally's wearing headphones at a listening station and tap her on the shoulder.

She slides off the headphones. "What?"

"I think we have a stalker," you joke. "Check out the front window . . . but don't look like you're looking!"

Mike peeks into the window again, and when he sees you and Sally staring right at him with smirks on your faces, he jumps out of the window frame like he's been stung.

Sally groans. "Boys are so stupid sometimes," she grouses, and then she hurries out of the store.

You follow around the other side of a top ten display, circling behind Mike's hiding spot so when you exit the store you're standing behind him, on the opposite side from Sally.

"Finding everything you need, Sir?" Sally asks Mike.

He stands up straight. "Uh . . . ," he says. "Do you work here now?"

"What are you talking about?" Sally snaps at him.

You tap Mike on the shoulder and grin at him when he whirls around to look at you. "She's joking," you inform him. "We were just shopping. Well . . . I was just checking out new releases that I might download later."

"That's illegal," Sally says, and both you and she giggle. "Mike, don't tell anyone she said that."

Mike doesn't turn to look at her but remains staring right at your face with a weird, confused expression in his eyes like he's having trouble focusing properly. "I already called the police on her," he says flatly.

It isn't until he smiles at you that you're entirely sure he's joking.

Oh, wow, his teeth are so white and perfectly set. He probably wore braces for years. You rub your tongue along the front of your own teeth, satisfied with their smoothly shaped curve. . . . It wasn't that long ago that you got your own braces taken off.

"That's okay," you reply to Mike, matching his deadpan tone. "I admit it — I've been naughty."

Mike coughs and laughs at the same time, sounding shocked and pleased, and you blush and smile.

"Me, too," Sally says. "I've been bad, too."

"I would never turn you in to the police," Mike tells you.

"How kind," you reply. "No matter what?"

"No matter what," Mike promises.

Sally makes a huffy noise and steps in front of Mike. "C'mon," she hisses at you. "We've got to go."

"Oh, yeah," you reply. Now you realize you've been staring right into Mike's stunning blue eyes, and you find yourself lost in figuring out the name of their exact color. *Azure? Cobalt? Robin's egg? Indigo? Sapphire? Sky? Cerulean? Swimming pool?* You shake your head, clearing it. "We've got to go," you tell Mike.

"I heard," he says.

"*Now.*" Sally seethes, yanking on your arm.

"Bye," you tell Mike.

"Bye," Mike says softly.

"B-Bye!" Sally snaps, and she pulls you toward the escalators. Once you're moving upward, she faces you. "What was that about?" she demands.

"What?" you ask nonchalantly.

She opens her mouth like she's about to tell you off, but no sound comes out. After a second, she lets out a long sigh. "Whatever," she says, sounding defeated. "It's not like it matters."

You both step off the escalator, and you have to hurry to keep up with Sally as she strides toward the food court. "Hold up," you call after her. "No, really . . . what?"

In front of Wok and Roll, she whirls around to glare at you. "I guess Mike and I are breaking up," she says.

"Really?" you ask. "Why do you say that?"

Sally shakes her head. "Don't pretend like you don't know," she says. "He's so into you, it's . . . it's almost creepy."

"I don't think so," you reply. "He's not into me. Mike's totally into you."

She laughs and gestures behind you. "Look," she says.

You turn around. Mike is standing on the far end of the mall's top level, watching you. When he sees you looking, he steps behind a cell phone kiosk, out of sight. After only a moment, he peers around the side, staring at you again. You can almost feel the intensity of his gaze from across the crowded shopping center.

"He's looking at you," you tell Sally. "You're his girl-friend."

"I don't think so," she says, crossing her arms. "That's all you. And I get it, it's fine, really. I don't care. He's never looked at me that way." She sniffles and tries to look brave. "I would never stand in the way of true love. If you're into him, go for it."

You're not completely sure that you're flattered by Mike's odd attention . . . especially since he's gawking at you right in full view of your best friend, whom he's supposed to be dating. Absolutely, no question, Mike is a hottie — even from across the mall, the way his dark hair falls onto his forehead makes your knees dangerously wobbly — but his staring routine is kind of a creep-out.

"So . . . ," Sally says, attempting to sound casual, "how do you feel about him?"

If you tell Sally that you're hot for Mike, turn to page 31. ➡

If you admit that you find him attractive, but that you've really lost any spark of interest you may have felt, turn to page 56. ➡

If you tell her sincerely that you were never into Mike, turn to page 17. ➡

If you tell her that you're not interested in him at all — even though you're not sure you mean it — turn to page 4. ➡

The next day is Saturday, and your mother is very surprised in the morning when you offer to drop off her weekly dry cleaning for her. Your dad is so impressed he even lends you his new sedan, which is excellent because his car's MP3 speaker system rocks.

When you get to the strip mall on Montgomery Avenue, you circle the parking lot twice until you're sure you've seen it — an old, champagne-colored BMW parked in front of Stan's Guitars. You swallow hard and realize that even though you volunteered for this errand, a big part of you was hoping you'd gotten the timing wrong and you wouldn't run into Mike. You park not far away, and sit in your car for about fifteen minutes until you're sure the coast is clear.

You go into the dry cleaner and hand over your parents' clothes. The dry cleaner guy has to keep repeating his questions because you're busy craning your neck to watch the parking lot out the window. Finally, as the clerk gives you tickets for the clothes, you give up and breathe a sigh of relief. You're not going to run into Mike — it just won't happen. So now you can go home and put to rest all your guilt about not being able to stop thinking about Sally's boyfriend.

You take only two steps into the parking lot before the

guitar store door opens and Mike steps out, carrying a big guitar case.

Should you run for it?

Don't be ridiculous. How rude would that be? You wave to him.

Mike spots you, smiles, waves back, and starts heading in your direction.

Maybe *now's* the time to run for it?

You feel so happy to see him.

"Hey," you say, "I was just dropping off some dry cleaning for my parents." You show him the pink ticket.

Mike nods and holds up the guitar case. "And I just finished a karate lesson," he jokes.You laugh, and he seems pleased. "No, I had a guitar lesson, of course," he says. "My hand's all sore because Stan's got me really trying to stretch my reach."

"What are you learning to play?" you ask.

"I've only learned some basic chords so far," Mike replies. He smiles. "So now I can play most of the stuff you hear on the radio."

"I'd love to hear you play sometime," you say. "You know, with Sally around or whatever. Oh yeah . . . how did the date go last night?" You've already heard Sally's full review — she called you as soon as she got home. According to her, Mike had been totally romantic, holding the car door open for her and buying her popcorn. They had even played with each other's fingers during the movie. But when he pulled up outside her house to drop her off at the end, both her parents came outside and waited on the front porch, so he could only give her a goodbye kiss on the cheek.

"It was good," Mike says. "We had fun. The movie was really cool, and Sally's great . . . but —"

Your throat goes dry. "But?"

He ducks his head and blushes a little. "No buts, I guess."

A silence falls between you, and you totally don't know what to say. "So . . ." you begin.

He swings his guitar and glances back toward his car. "So . . ." he repeats. "I . . . I was just going to head over to the park, maybe practice my guitar outside. It's a beautiful day. I know a great spot. For practicing guitar, I mean."

"Yeah?" you reply. "I was thinking of going to the park to take more pictures for the art show. I've got some good stuff, but I could always use more. Sometimes it's those pictures you take in a panic at the last minute that turn out the best."

"I know how that goes," Mike says. "So I'm going over there. You want to follow in your car?"

"Absolutely," you reply.

If you get into your car and follow him to the park, turn to page 54. ➡

If you get into your car and head home, standing him up, turn to page 153. ➡

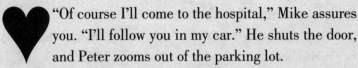"Of course I'll come to the hospital," Mike assures you. "I'll follow you in my car." He shuts the door, and Peter zooms out of the parking lot.

You glance back at Mike — he has a weird, big smile on his face as he waves to you.

Strange.

You can't think about that right now. You wrap your arms around your chest and press your lips together, trying not to cry.

Peter bangs his palms against the steering wheel. "What if she's —"

"Don't even say it," you interrupt. "Don't even think it."

"This is the most hideous thing ever," adds Sally, which really irritates you for some reason. You're glad of the annoyed feeling, and you try to focus on that, instead of on the horrible whirlpool of terror sucking at you, threatening to drown you in miserable panic.

Peter gets you to the hospital in record time, and the three of you rush into the emergency room. "Our mother was in a car accident!" Peter yells at the nurse on duty. "Where is she?"

The nurse peers up at Peter over her narrow glasses. "Calm down there. Yelling at me isn't going to help anything."

Sally pushes in front of Peter. "Okay," she tells the nurse, "their mother was in a car accident, and they're just really worried."

"I understand," the nurse says. She pulls a big register book toward her. "What's her name?"

You blurt out your mother's name, and the nurse slowly scans the book.

She reads over it again, running her finger down the names.

"She's not here," the nurse reports.

"This is the closest hospital," Peter says. "Would they have brought her to County? Isn't that too far?"

"She's got to be here," you say. "Check again."

"There haven't been any car accidents reported in the last hour," the nurse tells you primly.

You turn to face your brother. "What's going on?" you ask.

"I don't know," he says. "Call her."

"Who?" you ask. "Mom?"

"Yeah," Peter says. "Maybe a doctor or paramedics or someone will answer and we'll see where she is."

You pull out your phone and call your mother's number. Sally takes your hand and you squeeze hers, grateful for her support. The fluttering panic in your chest is making you feel horribly nauseous.

"Hello?" your mother answers.

Your eyes brim with tears at the sound of her voice. "Mom, where are you?" you blurt out. "Are you okay?"

"What's the matter?" your mother asks, freaking out herself when she hears your panic. "I'm home. What's going on? Are you all right? Where's Peter?"

"We're both here at the hospital," you tell her. "We're fine. We're looking for you."

"Why?" your mother asks. "What's going on? Tell me!"

"You were in a car accident," you explain.

"I was *what*?" your mother shoots back. "In a car accident? I haven't taken the car out all day."

"What's going on?" Peter demands to know. "Is she okay?"

You hand the phone to Peter, and you slump down onto one of the hard plastic emergency room chairs. Sally sits beside you, peering worriedly into your face.

"There was no accident," you say numbly.

"I don't understand," Sally says.

You totally feel like throwing up. "What other explanation is there?"

"For what?" Sally cries. "You're really freaking me out!"

"Mike's not here," you say. "He didn't follow us. There was no car accident."

Peter drops the phone. "No," he says.

"He said he was going to follow us," you repeat. "He didn't. He's not here."

Peter's face turns green. "The game," he says. "I'm missing the game."

"How could he do something like this?" you cry.

"I'm going to kill him," Peter says. "Or sue. This is fraud, isn't it? I can't believe this."

Tears are rolling down Sally's cheeks, and you realize your face is wet, too. "It's not possible," she whispers. "Nobody could be that mean."

"There's no other explanation," you say. You feel totally dead inside. Betrayed. Hurt on a level that you didn't even know was possible.

It's revenge, you think. Revenge on your brother for faking him out in the previous game. You have never felt so used. Deep below your cold fury about Mike's trickery is quiet relief that your mother is okay, but that's such a small emotion compared to the icy rage that's building inside you.

Mike isn't stupid. He was smart enough to completely fool you. He obviously never cared about you at all.

"He'd better watch his back," Peter mutters, sounding as deeply in shock and angry as you feel. "When I tell the other guys about what he did . . . he's dead meat."

"That won't bring back the playoffs," Sally adds unnecessarily. "I can't believe we believed him. I can't believe we trusted him!"

This betrayal is easily the crappiest maneuver anyone's ever done to you in your whole life.

It's insanely mean and evil at base level, but it feels so much worse because of the excruciating curdling in your heart.

Guys can be so cruel.

The End.

Ten minutes later, you and Mike are sitting on opposite ends of the top of a picnic table in the park, and he has his guitar out between you. You're holding your camera in your hand, wrapping the wrist strap around your finger tightly.

"This is a song I'm writing for Sally," Mike says. He strums the strings a few times and then starts picking out notes. It doesn't really sound like anything except random plinking. "Wait," he says, and he starts over with the strumming again, sticking out his tongue in concentration. It doesn't sound anything like what he just played, except that it seems completely random again.

"*Sally,*" he suddenly starts to sing totally off key, "*the prettiest girl in the valley. Oh, Sally . . . you're right up my alley —*"

You burst out laughing. "You're kidding, right?" you gasp.

For a second, Mike looks hurt, but then he starts laughing, too. "C'mon," he protests. "I'm just *learning.* Today was only my third lesson!"

"I'm sure you'll get better soon," you say, still chuckling a little. "But for now, don't play in public yet. Stick to sports."

"That's harsh," Mike says, smiling. He puts the guitar down on the picnic table. "So you think I'm just a dumb jock, huh? Well, I prefer to consider myself a natural athlete. Check this out."

He takes a deep breath, runs a little onto the park lawn, performs a perfect cartwheel, and then instantly flips himself onto his hands and holds himself up in a very straight handstand.

You applaud and then lift up your camera. "Hold that pose!" you order him.

But you wait until his face is red and his arms are trembling before you take the shot. "Got it!" you call out, and Mike collapses onto the grass.

He quickly bounces up again, though, and launches himself into a back flip. Now you really are impressed, and you whistle loudly. Mike grins at you as he starts doing weight-lifting poses for you, flexing his long, skinny soccer muscles.

Watching him show off for you makes your whole body feel light and sunny, constantly on the verge of giggling. His tight T-shirt stretches over his muscles.

He's so cute.

If you ask Mike to keep modeling for you, turn to page 68. ➡

If you put down your camera and join Mike performing park gymnastics, turn to page 115. ➡

♥ Funny, the moment Sally admits that she's lost interest in Mike, your feelings for him fizzle out too.

You know he's good-looking, but now you can't even remember what the rush of attraction for him felt like anymore.

It's really not that interesting to consider crushing on one of Sally's castoffs.

You have always prided yourself on being a good judge of character, and on having better taste in guys than Sally.

What good is a guy even she wouldn't date?

The End.

Something about the guarded way Mike holds himself — his face stern, his shoulders back in a strong posture — makes you think he wouldn't enjoy seeing a photo of himself getting faked out on the field. Yeah, you really get the feeling he wouldn't be into seeing that at all.

Anyway, why focus on the bad stuff?

"You've got some great moves out there," you tell him. "You look like you've been a soccer star your whole life, like before you could even *walk*."

Over Mike's head, Sally shoots you a look. Maybe you were laying it on a bit thick.

Your big compliments don't bother Mike, though. "You know it," he replies. "My dad almost went pro way back in the early eighties, but that was before America was paying any attention to the sport, so there weren't any opportunities for him. He was my first coach. So, yeah, I have played soccer since I could walk." He takes a swig off a sports water bottle, washes it around in his mouth, and then spits neatly off to the side. "It's just something I do naturally. Like, genetically."

"Cool," you say, feeling pleased that you were on target with your observation.

"No surprise there!" Sally chirps, overly enthusiastic. She puts her hands on Mike's shoulders. "Anyone can tell you've got tons of experience. It's *obvious* the whole team is built around you."

After years of hanging around with Sally every day, sometimes you think you know her too well — you can see right through her little attempt to stay on top. She's always trying to one-up people, but she rarely tries that with you. You're surprised how much it stings.

Mike laughs and stands up off the bench. He faces Sally and pulls her close. "You're crazy," he tells her. "You're already crazy in love with me. You can't hide it at all, crazy girl."

As Sally giggles and blushes with her arms around Mike's sweaty waist, you look away . . . and try to figure out why you feel so annoyed. Yeah, Mike's ego is the size of Godzilla, but that's not necessarily a bad thing, at least not entirely. Confident guys can be hot. Even arrogance can be sexy sometimes . . . if it's backed up by the goods.

Maybe it's that you can't believe Mike's falling for Sally's girly-girl show. Can't he tell it's all an act? For some reason, you just can't get it through your head that guys *always* fall for the Barbie doll fairy princess.

Now Sally sits down hard on Mike's lap, squishing his soccer shorts.

"Oof," he says softly.

Sally giggles, throwing an arm around Mike's neck to

stabilize herself on top of him. For someone so pretty, Sally can come off as a desperate flirt sometimes.

You're not being fair. Sally is your very best friend. You and she have always been honest in your critiques and compliments of one another. She's got a more made-up look, but you also put a lot of thought into your appearance. You've practiced your flirting techniques, too, so you should cut her some slack.

You notice that Sally's wearing a new necklace — a small, flat pink oval in a gold frame. You sit down next to Mike on the bench and reach into their love knot to gently raise the pendant up from Sally's throat. The pink oval is a slim slice of rose quartz, marbleized with fine white lines. "Nice," you say.

"It's supposed to give me emotional stability," she says with a little laugh. "Rose quartz is good for that."

"You can't believe that crap," Mike says. When Sally shrugs, he gives her a squeeze and tickles her a little. She squeals and squirms in his arms, and Mike leans toward you. The edge of his shoulder pushes into your upper arm. He doesn't pull away quickly from the contact. Is he keeping his shoulder pressed against you for a heartbeat too long? After Sally stops squirming and he shifts away from you, the sensation where he touched you lingers like an echo.

"Okay," you say, standing up. "There's nowhere I've got to be, but I'm done with this place."

Mike drums on Sally's back for a second. "Up!" he says, and she climbs to her feet, too.

"We're going to a party tonight," Sally brags to you.

"What happened to the movie plans?" you ask.

"Nixed," Sally answers. "Who wants to go to some dumb action flick, anyway? I'd much rather go to a party in a mansion."

"In a *mansion*," you reply. "Ooh la la."

"It's up in the hills and has a view of the whole town," she continues cheerfully. "Mike knows some kid whose parents are in Hawaii." She shoves Mike's shoulder. "Hey, what was that kid's name again?"

Mike raises his eyebrows at the shove, pauses a second, and then returns to stuffing a towel into his gym bag. "Darren."

"Darren," Sally tells you. "His dad's a banker or something rich and boring like that, but Mike says Darren throws good parties."

"Have fun," you say. "I'm going to catch up on my needlepoint." That's a joke. You'll probably really just watch TV.

Sally laughs. "Well, I wish you could come with us," she says.

Mike zips up his gym bag and stands up. "Why can't she?" he asks.

"Because," Sally replies, a little annoyed by his denseness, "I thought invitations were hard to get."

60

"Nah," Mike says, smiling. "Darren said we could bring anyone we wanted. She should come."

"She doesn't *want* to come," Sally says firmly. "Needle-point, etc."

"Go ahead," you say. "Talk about me like I'm not here."

"You can never have too many girls at a party," Mike explains. "She should come." He looks at you with those potent blue eyes that make you forget what you're thinking about. "You should come."

Sally glares at you over Mike's shoulder, a big, fat *No!* blazing in her eyes.

"I don't think so," you say.

"You're going to leave me hanging?" Mike asks. "The girl/boy ratio will be a mess if you don't come. You're coming."

Sally glances at him sharply. You understand that she wants to be alone with Mike, but the implied disses of you are irritating.

"She's your best friend. You should want her there, and the party needs her," Mike tells Sally in an extremely final tone. "She's coming."

Sally's too sensitive not to pick up on the dangerous edge in his voice — he's threatening to be angry with her if she doesn't listen to him. Which is the opposite of what she wants. Especially since they've been dating only a week.

"Oh, come along," she says to you with a giant smile,

acting like that's what she wanted the whole time. "We'll all have fun. Maybe you'll even meet someone there!"

You have a feeling that Mike doesn't just want you to come simply because the party needs girls. It's more complicated than that — *he's* more complex than that. Mike's been vibing you since the moment you shook hands, and there's really no getting around the fact that he's entirely hot. Yeah, his high opinion of himself is bothersome, but you admit that if he wasn't Sally's boyfriend, you would totally want to get to know him better.

But he is Sally's boyfriend.

Do you really want to provoke a dangerous drama between Sally and you with Mike in the middle? How big a mess would *that* be?

If you think going to the party just might be worth the trouble, turn to page 121. ➡

If playing third wheel at a party with strange guys and not enough girls isn't your idea of a good time, turn to page 163. ➡

♥ Even feeling desperate, you know there's no reason you should ruin Mike's chances in the playoffs, too.

"Thank you," you tell him, and you shut the door a second before Peter steps on the gas and the car screeches out of the parking lot.

As he pulls into the street, you glance back. Mike is standing still on the asphalt, watching your car leave. You start to sob in the front seat of the car.

"No," Peter says. "I've got to drive. Don't lose it on me, okay? This is already too messed up."

Sally hugs you from behind, around the back of the seat. "It'll be okay," she tells you. "It will be all right."

But what if it isn't? What if your mother isn't all right?

Peter parks in the hospital lot and the three of you race inside. An orderly tells you how to get to the emergency area.

You all run up to the nurse on duty in the emergency room. "Our mother," Peter gasps, "was in a car accident." The fluorescent lights in the room are harsh and glaring, and your eyes are smarting, your vision broken up into blurry fragments.

"Yes," the nurse says calmly. She's a pretty, petite woman with kind brown eyes. "She came in a little while ago. The paramedics had already stabilized her on the way here.

Luckily, they were nearby when they got the call about the accident."

Sally hugs you.

"What does that mean?" you ask the nurse over Sally's shoulder.

"Your mother will be fine," the nurse tells you. "She has a mild concussion and a few bruises, but she'll be fine."

"Can we see her?" you ask.

"I'll tell the doctor you're here," the nurse replies. "When he says it's okay for you to see her, I'll bring you to her. In the meantime, have a seat, okay?"

"Okay," you say. "Okay."

Sally lets go of you, and you slump down into a plastic seat in the waiting room. You take a deep, ragged breath, and put your head down between your knees for a long moment.

When you raise your head again, you're already in so much shock that it barely registers in your brain that Sally is wrapped in your brother's arms, and they're kissing.

"Whoa," you say. "What?"

Peter slowly pulls away from Sally. "I'm going to get a drink from the soda machine," he says, and he stalks off down the hall.

Sally slowly walks over and sits down beside you. "I think I've got something to tell you," she says.

"Apparently," you reply. "Obviously." A part of you knows that Sally kissing Peter should be a big deal, but at the moment you feel too relieved about your mother to really grasp what's going on with your best friend and your brother.

"I'm sorry I didn't tell you right away," Sally blurts out. "I was never really into Mike. Even though they're on opposite teams, Mike's a friend of Peter's, and Mike agreed to let you think that I was into him because —"

"Because you thought I'd be against you and Peter?" you ask.

"Exactly!" Sally says. "You're always saying how you don't want to hear about my feelings for Peter, so we hid it from you and used Mike as a smokescreen. I'm sorry. When this thing happened with your mother, I couldn't hide it anymore, and I'm sorry. I didn't mean —"

You wave your hand for her to stop talking. "Peter's into you too?" you ask.

"Yes," Sally replies. "Really and truly."

You sigh. "It wasn't that I didn't want you two to be together," you explain. "That wasn't it." You let out a little, rueful laugh. "I was just tired of hearing you moan about your crush."

Sally laughs, too, and hugs you. "So you're okay with this?" she asks. "You sure?"

"I'm sure," you say. You gesture toward the nurse. "It's not a big deal, especially in the scheme of things, you know?"

"I know," Sally whispers, and she hugs you again.

Your brain feels kind of scrambled from the scare about your mother, and you don't feel quite at ease yet. . . . You won't, until you see that she's safe and sound. Under all your confusion, though, it dawns on you what it means that Sally was never interested in Mike.

There are no strings to keep you from dating him.

"I've got something to tell you, too," you say to Sally.

Sally smiles. "Mike?" she asks.

"How did you know?" you answer.

She nods her head toward the emergency room entrance.

Mike is standing in the doorway, looking around. When he spots you, he rushes over.

"You're okay with that?" you ask Sally.

"I'm happy for you," Sally says.

Peter shows up holding sodas, and Sally gets up to join him.

"Relax," you tell Mike. "My mother's going to be fine. The nurse said it was only a mild concussion and some bruises. Thank you so much for letting us know."

Mike takes your hand and holds it in both of his. He glances up at Sally and Peter, who are holding one another again on the other side of the emergency room. "I'm sorry I couldn't tell you everything," he says. "I made a promise. It sucked not being able to tell you that Sally and I weren't together. I hated lying to you. It's just . . . me falling for you wasn't part of the plan."

"It's cool," you say. "I'm so glad you're here."

You lean toward Mike, and he holds you in his arms. Pressed against his chest, you can't help but notice how perfectly you fit within his embrace.

The End.

♥You stand up on the grass and hold your camera up. "If you're going to model for me, let's do this right," you say fake-sternly, with a hint of a bogus European accent. "Show me attitude! It's all about attitude."

Mike stiffens like a mannequin and sticks his nose up in the air, acting all haughty as he holds overly-serious modeling poses.

"That's right, baby!" you call, snapping photos and trying not to giggle and ruin the act. "Now give me *passion*, give me . . . *animal*. You're a tiger, baby!"

Mike holds up his hands like claws. "Rarr," he says limply.

You can't stop laughing. It's hard to even take the picture. You fall to the ground and sit on one hip, still giggling. Mike's laughing, too, and he collapses on the grass, rolling around. You take some excellent close-up photos of him cracking up, the blades of bright green grass framing his laughing, adorable face.

With a deep, long breath, you realize you haven't laughed that hard since you tried on your grandmother's old wigs with Sally —

Oh. Sally. An icky rush of guilt overwhelms you and you sit up straight, lowering your camera.

Mike's lying flat on his back, chewing on the end of a long grass stalk. "Hey, doesn't that cloud look like a tiger?" he asks. "The one above that maple tree?"

"Yeah," you reply, not even looking up. You should not be cloud-watching with Sally's boyfriend. That's way too romantic and wrong. "Listen," you say, trying to think up an excuse to escape. "I've got to go, okay? There's this thing I have to do for my parents. It's stupid, but I promised. . . ."

Mike puts his hands behind his head and turns to smile at you. His smile is so dazzling you see spots like you accidentally looked directly at the sun. "Sure," Mike says casually. "Catch you later."

All day Sunday, you develop your photos and sort through them, wondering which four you're going to enter in the show tomorrow night. You decide on two shots of the river and two gorgeous pictures of Sally. While you're framing those pictures, you take a lot of breaks to stare at the photos you took of Mike modeling, roaring, and laughing, but each time you force yourself away, close the files, and get back to preparing your exhibit.

You should force yourself never to look at Mike again — in photos, or in person.

By Monday, you've almost forgotten about Mike in your excitement about the show. After school, you rush home and get dressed to the nines in an elegant black dress and heels. You wear your hair up, and your mother lends you a gorgeous silver necklace with a single perfect pearl hanging from it. You feel completely sophisticated as your parents drive you over to city hall, although you do have a little trouble with your heels when you try to climb the steep marble stairs in front of the building.

Inside, the reception hall where the art has been hung is teeming with well-dressed students and their parents, teachers, art lovers, and city council members. You knew being chosen for this show was a big deal, but you didn't know it was *this* big a deal! There are even newspaper and magazine reporters in the room!

Your photography teacher, Ms. Adams, comes over to congratulate you and meet your parents. While they're chatting, you spot Sally in the crowd. You excuse yourself and make your way toward your best friend.

"Sal!" you call.

Sally squeals and grabs your hands. "It's amazing," she gushes at you. "You take the best pictures ever — I can't even believe how talented you are. I never thought I could look that good! *Never.* I really look like a model."

"You could be a model if that's what you want to do," you tell her sincerely. You mean it — you've taken hundreds of pictures of her over the years, and Sally seems incapable of looking bad in any of them.

"And the pictures of the river in the woods," Sally continues. "They're so mysterious . . . like a fairy tale!"

"Totally," says a deep voice behind you. Mike steps around you and puts his arm around Sally's shoulders. "Those river pictures make me feel like I'm lost in an amazing but kind of scary folktale. They look like the *old country*, or something. Like there isn't a city in a thousand miles of that place."

"Thanks," you say, trying not to blush. Mike one-hundred percent nailed what you were trying to show, so perfectly it's like he read your mind.

"Exactly," Sally adds. "Stay here. I'm going to get us some punch."

"I'll go," Mike offers.

"No, let me," Sally says. "There's someone I want to talk to over there anyway. I'll be right back."

With Sally gone, Mike just stares at you for a long moment, and you glance around awkwardly, wondering what you should say to him.

"I like the river photos," Mike says softly, "but I love the ones of Sally. It's like you saw inside her and showed us the best part of her . . . the beauty within as much as the beauty outside. They're both really amazing pictures."

"Thank you," you say.

But really, you're not sure if he's praising your photography talent, or if he's just letting you know how perfect he thinks Sally is.

If you decide he's praising your talent and you want to keep talking to him, turn to page 77. ➤

If you decide he's praising Sally's beauty and you shouldn't have anything more to do with him, turn to page 142. ➤

The next week seems to last forever. Sally did indeed dump Mike, and they agreed to just be friends with no hard feelings, but you haven't quite gotten up the nerve to tell her that you and Mike are an item now.

Unfortunately, Mike can't see you during the week because he's busy with soccer practice, but you get one good IM conversation with him on Wednesday. He's not a great typist, but he does tell you that he's looking forward to seeing you at the big game, which echoes in your head all day Thursday and Friday.

Saturday afternoon finally arrives, and Sally shows up at your house. You'd almost forgotten that you and she are getting a ride from Peter to the game. You take a deep breath as you all climb into Peter's car, preparing to act cool all afternoon so Sally doesn't suspect that you're into Mike.

It's too soon to tell her the truth.

"What's wrong?" Sally asks you as Peter pulls into the school parking lot. "You've barely said a word since I got to your house."

"It's nothing," you say. "I'm just nervous about the game, and a little tired."

"It's just a stupid soccer game," Sally replies.

"There's no such thing as a stupid soccer game," Peter says as he cuts the engine. "Only stupid players." He slips on his lucky headband before he opens the car door.

"Whatever," you say. "At least I'll get some good photos for the paper."

As you open your door, the first thing you see is Mike running across the parking lot toward you, his face flushed.

All your emotional alarms go off. You know that when Sally sees you with Mike, she's going to know everything instantly.

You've got to come clean now. You grab Sally's arm and she whirls around to face you, looking confused. "Sal," you say, "I didn't mean to do anything that —"

"It's your mother!" Mike hollers.

You drop Sally's arm and stare at Mike. All the blood has drained from his face now, and you realize that something horrible has happened. Your stomach drops. "My mother?" you ask.

Mike gasps for air. "On my way over," he pants, "I saw a car accident."

Peter appears behind you, holding your shoulder a little too hard. "What's going on?" he demands to know.

"I saw your mother in an accident," Mike says, holding his side. "She has a white Ford, right?"

"Oh, no," Sally says.

You feel as though you might faint. "What happened?" you cry.

"I saw your mom being loaded onto a stretcher," Mike continues. "Into an ambulance. The paramedics took her to the hospital."

Peter lets go of you, rushes around to the driver's side of his car, and yanks the door open. "Let's go," he says. "Get in."

Without Peter supporting you, your knees buckle, and Sally grabs you around the waist, holding you up.

"What about the game?" Sally asks.

"What does that matter?" Peter yells back. "We have to get to the hospital now!"

"I'm coming, too," Sally says. She opens the passenger side.

"I don't believe this," you say. "This can't be happening."

"Go on," Mike urges you gently. "Go to the hospital with Sally and your brother."

You nod and let him help you into the car.

Even in your shocked state, you can't help noticing how sweet Mike is being to you. It makes you want to burst into tears. You don't want him to leave your side. You're so scared, and him being near you is the only thing stopping you from totally losing it.

Should you ask him to come with you to the hospital, too?

If you realize that there's no reason Mike should miss the game, too, so you don't ask him to come with you, turn to page 63. ➡

If you realize that you need Mike now and you ask him to please come with you, turn to page 49. ➡

♥ You stand next to Mike and regard your photos critically. "I like these shots," you tell Mike, "but sometimes they seem too *posed* to me."

"Too posed?" Mike asks. "How can a river be posed? It's rushing downstream."

"Maybe *posed* isn't the right word," you say. You're silent a moment, trying to figure out how to explain what you mean. It's nice being silent next to Mike — he's obviously considerate enough to give you time to think, and you don't feel rushed or awkward at all. "Maybe I mean *imposed*," you say. "Like I knew what meaning I was trying to reach for, and so I forced that into the picture, when really the photo should speak for itself. So maybe that makes the shot feel kind of fake."

"I don't think they're fake at all," Mike argues. "I like them. I think they show a pure vision. Which can only come from a pure heart."

You glance up at him. His face is totally serious, as if daring you to laugh at the earnest things he said about your photos. Saying your heart is pure is kind of cheesy, but you find it touching, too. "That's sweet," you say.

"I meant every word," Mike replies.

Sally pushes between you, oblivious to your conversation

with Mike. "You're not going to believe this," she gushes. "It's totally incredible, like beyond words. That guy I was talking to over by the food table? He's a talent scout for *Flair Modeling Agency*. And because of your pictures, he's interested in me! The Flair Modeling Agency is interested in *me*!"

"That's so cool!" you tell Sally. "I'm so, so happy for you." You give her a big hug, and the two of you jump up and down together, squealing in excitement. Sally and you have been talking almost your whole lives about your pictures making her famous . . . and now that dream is coming true!

"Okay, play it cool," says Sally. She lets you go, and you both regain your composure. Then Sally hugs you again. "I'm never going to forget you doing this for me," she tells you sincerely. "When I become a supermodel and I can demand whatever I want, I'm only going to let you take my pictures."

"You're the best," you say. "You totally deserve this."

"I said you could be a model, didn't I?" Mike adds.

Sally whirls around and grabs Mike in an enormous hug, pressing her cheek against his chest. "You are the most supportive boyfriend ever!" she cheers. "You're my rock."

You can't help chuckling a little at Sally's dramatics. Oh, sure, Mike's her rock — she hasn't even known him for two weeks yet. But, whatever, you're happy for her.

"So what should we do now?" Mike asks.

Sally turns to face you, but keeps one arm around Mike's torso, unwilling to break the hug. She winks at you. "My rock is going to take me out to celebrate."

"I am?"

"You are."

"Who am I to argue?" Mike says. "I'm just a rock."

As Mike starts to lead Sally away through the crowd, she turns back to you. "Are you cool with me leaving?" she asks. "You'll be okay, yes?"

You wave her away. "I'm fine," you tell her. "I'm enjoying my moment in the sun."

Sally beams her brightest smile at you. "Call me," she says.

"I will," you promise, and then she disappears into the crowd.

What does it mean that Mike didn't even turn around to say good-bye to you?

It means that he's Sally's boyfriend, and you should remember that fact.

After the art show ends, your parents take you home, and you quickly get out of your constricting dress and pinching heels and throw on comfy sweatpants and a T-shirt. You plop down on a beanbag in your room and sink into it, relaxing.

It was a perfect evening. Your photos were a big hit, and even strangers came up to you with insightful things to say about them. It was so much fun being treated like a real art photographer, for the first time ever. Your parents and Ms. Adams were so proud. Then Sally got noticed by Flair . . . which is like the coolest thing ever. You've barely ever seen her happier than she was tonight.

And Mike . . .

What about Mike?

He's got you so confused. On the one hand, standing next to him and talking about your photos, you felt like some part of you that had been sleeping your whole life was suddenly waking up. You love the way you sound when you're with him. You love the way he seems to see you, the way he trusts you with his thoughts.

On the other hand, he's probably totally in love with your best friend, who is beautiful enough to become a model.

That's a wall you just can't get around, the fact that he's Sally's boyfriend.

Sally and Mike should be home from their celebration by now, you figure. It's a Monday night — they couldn't have stayed out too late. You promised to give Sally a call, but with all those thoughts about Mike spinning in your head, you're not sure you want to talk to her right now.

If you do your duty as a best friend and call her, turn to page 85. ➤

If you decide to call Sally later, and instead go for a walk now to clear your head, turn to page 94. ➤

There are many reasons why you should not kiss Mike.

But as he leans forward, your entire range of vision tunnels down to a single point of focus — his lips, getting closer to yours. Such beautiful lips, a purplish red like raspberries. At the last second, you close your eyes and totally give in to his kiss.

Oh, it's good. The taste of his lips is amazingly sweet, even beyond the flavor of the sugary iced tea. Ever so gently, his lips brush against yours, tingling as they push together, the sensation lingering as they pull apart.

You sit back and lick your lips, afraid to look Mike in the eyes, still reeling from the intensity of the kiss.

He should not be kissing you. Sure, Sally told you she's lost interest in him, but he doesn't know that!

Mike shifts to the edge of his seat, closer to you, pressing his knees in between yours. "You look so pretty right now," he whispers.

Something deep inside you softens, a dangerous ooze of emotion. "Thank you," you reply softly, your lips inches from his.

"Enjoying the sandwiches?" your mother asks.

You and Mike jump apart, back against your chairs.

Your mother laughs and turns away to work on her garden again.

"Uh . . . I've got to go," Mike says.

"Yeah," you say. "I'll walk you out."

As you lead Mike back through the house, you pass your living room, where your brother is now slumped on the couch, watching TV. Peter raises his eyebrows and sits up a little when he sees Mike.

"Hey," Mike says.

"Hey," Peter replies, and then he slumps back down and turns up the volume with the remote.

At the front door, Mike leans down to whisper in your ear. "Your brother's a loser," he says. "We're going to destroy him in the playoffs."

You just stand in shock as you watch Mike walk back to his car.

Did he really just say that to you?

If you decide to cut Mike some slack — he and your brother are on rival teams, after all, and boys get crazy about sports — turn to page 73. ➡

If you think that's just too rude and your interest in Mike goes completely cold, turn to page 120. ➡

The whole next day, you do basically nothing but get ready for the evening bowling with Mike. The only tricky moment is a phone call you get from Sally asking if you want to hang out that night, but you tell her you have to stay in to finish a paper you've totally been putting off.

By the time you're ready to leave — only a few minutes late — you're so worked up and excited about meeting Mike that you have to roll down your windows as you drive so you don't overheat.

You park your car and stride into Kingpin Lanes. With your new tight sweater and cute pants, you know you look good, and you can't wait for Mike to get a look at you. It's not like boys ever notice shoes, but yours are so perfect for your outfit that they fill you with self-confidence anyway — even if you'll have to change into bowling shoes pretty soon.

Quickly, you spot Mike. He's sitting on a bench with his head down. You rush over to him, but halfway there you remember to act cool, and you slow down and walk toward him normally.

"Hi," you say.

Mike glances up, and you're immediately startled by the worried look on his face. "Hi," he says tightly.

"What's the matter?" you ask.

"What are you doing here?" asks a familiar voice behind you.

Sally's voice.

You stiffen and turn around slowly to face her. What can you possibly say to explain? She looks extraordinarily pretty, even by her high standards, and all of a sudden you're drawing a complete blank about what to say to her. You start feeling panicky.

Sally is confused to see you at Kingpin Lanes — although she's still acting cheerful, you can tell that she's picking up on your nervous vibe. "What are you *doing* here?" she asks again.

Funny, that's exactly the same question you want to ask her.

If you try to make up a quick excuse to tell Sally, turn to page 218. ➡️

If you decide to fight for your man and say, "I have a date with Mike," turn to page 208. ➡️

♥ When you call Sally's cell phone, her mother answers. "Oh, thank goodness you called," she tells you. "See if you can figure out what's the matter with her. She won't tell me anything."

In the background, you hear, "Mom, give me that!"

"Are you all right?" you ask as soon as you hear Sally take control of the phone.

Sally immediately starts sobbing into the receiver. "Hold on," she gasps at you. "No, Mom!" you hear her shout in the background. "Leave me alone!" Then a door slams, and a second later, Sally is weeping into the phone again.

"What's going on?" you beg her to tell you. "Did something happen? You're scaring me!"

"I'm so ashamed!" Sally wails. "I'm so stupid!"

"Sally, tell me what happened!" you demand.

"It's Mike," she sobs. "We were having such an awesome evening — it was totally the best night of my life. But then he admitted to me . . . he admitted that he's seeing someone else!"

Oh, no. You stiffen in fear. What did Mike tell her? Did he tell her about when you almost kissed him?

Part of you is terrified about what Sally's going to do now — if she's going to trash your friendship with her forever. You can't think of any good excuses to tell her to make her forgive you. You know deep down that it was really sleazy to let your feelings for her boyfriend get out of control.

But there's another part of you that's happy to have the whole thing with Mike out in the open now. Hiding your feelings for him was so stressful, and you are not pleased with the dark circles that are forming under your eyes because of all the tension. You sigh with relief. If Mike decided to confess everything to Sally, that must mean he's chosen to be with *you*.

"I'm so sorry —" you begin.

"It's some horrible blonde from his chemistry class!" Sally cries. "His new *lab partner*! Isn't that classic? Isn't that the most classic thing you've ever heard in your life?"

This news hits you so hard, you almost drop the phone. "His lab partner?" you repeat in shock. "A classic blonde?" Your stomach turns over, and you almost feel the need to be sick. You are not Mike's lab partner, nor are you a blonde.

Not only was Mike trying to cheat on Sally with you . . . he was also cheating on both of you with some skank in his chemistry class!

You can't believe you were falling for that slimeball.

"Listen to me," you tell Sally firmly, "forget about him, okay? He's pond scum. This has nothing to do with you, and everything to do with how big a sleaze Mike is."

"I loved him," Sally sobs. "My heart is broken."

"I know, sweetie, I know," you whisper. You sigh deeply

to yourself, willing yourself not to cry, too. You do know exactly how she's feeling, because your heart is aching in the same way, but you can't tell her that.

How could you ever have considered inflicting this kind of pain on your best friend by going after her boyfriend? It's heartrending, the depth of Sally's pain. You know that you'll never try to steal anyone's boyfriend ever again.

"Put him out of your mind," you tell Sally, gritting your teeth in anger. "Don't give him the satisfaction of crying over him. Just forget about him, because he was never in your league, and he didn't deserve you for a second."

"I know," Sally says. She blows her nose, but still sounds sniffly when she comes back on the phone. "You're my best friend, and I love you," she says. "You know that, right?"

"I know it," you tell her. "I love you, too. We'll get over this, you and me together."

You will not give Mike another thought. Right now, your best friend in the world is miserable, shattered into a million pieces, and she needs your help pulling herself back together again.

But who will mend the crushed pieces of *your* broken heart?

The End.

When you ask yourself, *Do I like Mike?*, a strong, positive answer pops up: *yes.* Yes. Really, how can you doubt it? You haven't stopped thinking about him from the moment you saw him on the soccer field.

As you get ready for bed, you think about all the problems this realization will cause. Sally says she's over him, but it's still not cool for you to move in so quickly. What's the acceptable waiting period before you're allowed to date your best friend's ex? *Is* there an acceptable waiting period, or is it always forbidden?

It's not fair, you think while you brush your teeth. Under normal circumstances, the first thing you would do would be to call Sally and hash all of this out with her. It makes you feel just awful that there's a part of your thoughts you two can't share.

As you snuggle down under your covers, you have to face the biggest question of all.

Okay, good, you know you like Mike.

But you don't know if he likes you.

You're still thinking about Mike the next afternoon while you're helping your mother stake up the tomato plants in her small garden patch in the back yard. You are thinking how attraction is just like a tomato vine — it reaches out its tender little tendrils and clings to the person you desire, climbing up and getting stronger as it grows toward the sun — when you faintly hear the doorbell ring inside the house.

"I'll get it," you tell your mom, and you brush off your hands and head into the house.

When you open the door, Mike is standing on your front porch.

Like you conjured him up out of thin air by obsessing over him.

"Hey," he says.

"Hi," you say.

"Uh . . . I never do this," Mike tells you. He pulls a big orange Gerber daisy out from behind his back. "I brought this for you."

"Wow," you say, and that's pretty much all you're thinking, too — *wow*. "Thanks." You take the flower and sniff it. It has no smell whatsoever except a flat waxiness. "That's really nice of you."

"It's cool," Mike says. "I mean, you're welcome. It doesn't have to be a big deal."

"It's a very pretty flower," you tell him. You push the door open wide. "Come on," you say. "I was working in the yard with my mom — come on back."

"Okay," Mike replies, and he follows you into the house.

As you walk through your kitchen, you glance back at him and smile. It's so strange to see him there, next to your refrigerator. He seems too big or something, like he's not quite real.

"You're not going to make me do any yard work, are you?" Mike asks. "I just finished mowing my own lawn this morning."

"Everything's mowed," you reply as you step onto the tile outside the kitchen door. "We're just working in the garden."

You stop short when you see your mom on her knees in the middle of the tomato plants, leaning over to push a stake in the ground. Her butt looks enormous sticking up in the air, and it suddenly dawns on you that *you just led Mike right to your mother*. You have a sudden urge to push him back in the house and pretend like this never happened. Thank goodness your dad is out somewhere — he gets so freaky about boys visiting you.

Your mother sits up. "Oh," she says, pushing a strand of hair back behind her ear. "Who's this?"

"I'm Mike," he says, stepping forward to shake her hand.

"He's a friend of Sally's," you say. "It's complicated."

"Nice daisy," your mother says. She stands up and brushes dirt off her knees. "You kids go sit in the gazebo. I'll bring you out a snack."

She goes into the house, and you lead Mike toward the far corner of the yard, where your mother has set up a small gazebo surrounded by vine-covered trellises. In the gazebo is a little white wrought-iron table with two matching chairs.

Mike glances around nervously as he takes a seat. He looks really out of place in your mother's fancy garden, and the plain orange jersey he's wearing stands out like a hunter's vest in the woods. Although it does accentuate his shoulders nicely. "Someone put in a lot of work back here," he says.

"My mother designed it all," you reply, sitting down across from him. You put the daisy down on the table. "I'm just the slave labor that has to help her take care of it."

He laughs, still sounding nervous, and looks around at the various patches of flowers and rock formations and ceramic figurines of woodland creatures. "It's really . . . busy."

As your mother comes out the back door carrying a tea tray, you have a moment of looking at the backyard like Mike must be seeing it. It looks . . . uptight. Fussy.

You shift the daisy to give your mother room to put down the tea tray on the table. It's amazing how quickly she whipped up tiny sandwiches and glasses of iced tea . . . but she's always been kind of an intimidating, perfect hostess.

"Uh," says Mike. "I wasn't planning on staying long."

"Nonsense," your mother tells him. "It's not every day when a handsome young man shows up at our front door with a beautiful flower for my daughter."

Your stomach clenches. *"Mom,"* you say.

She just smiles at your embarrassment. She totally said that on purpose to make you squirm.

"Yeah," Mike says. He glances around the garden again,

staring at the white trellis behind your mother which is covered with an intricate web of blooming morning glories. "Uh . . . unbelievable backyard," he says. "It's like . . . a cheesy wedding cake or something."

Your mother's smile disappears instantly. "Oh," she says softly. "Well, yes, I suppose."

Mike couldn't know how important this yard is to her, how many hours she spends out there working on it, but still, her feelings are hurt. It makes you feel icky inside that Mike mocked her work so thoughtlessly. He doesn't seem to notice and grabs a little tuna sandwich.

"Enjoy," your mother says, and she heads into the house.

"Your mom's kind of weird and old-fashioned, huh," Mike observes.

You have no idea how to respond. He just insulted your mother *again*. Even if you agree with him, it's not his place to say it. "What made you decide to stop by?" you ask, changing the subject.

Mike grips the edge of the metal table with both hands. "All morning I was thinking about you," he says softly. He almost sounds angry, and his face turns red. "I was thinking about kissing you."

"Oh, yeah?" you ask, your mouth going dry.

"Yeah," Mike says, and suddenly he leans forward for a kiss.

If you decide to ignore his accidental insults and give him a quick kiss, turn to page 81. ➡

If you decide that dumb, pretty, and sweet you could handle, but you're not interested in a guy who's dumb and thoughtlessly mean, so you send Mike home, turn to page 120. ➡

The exciting events of the evening have got you in a bit of a tizzy, so you pull on a light jacket and go for a walk down the street. Not far from your house is a cute street with quaint shops and restaurants, and you head that way, enjoying the crisp night air.

There are a few other people strolling around the shopping area, although most of the stores are closed. You spend a few minutes looking at some decent photos in a little storefront gallery, and when you turn to continue down the block, you see a familiar figure walking your way.

It's Mike, and he's alone.

Any thoughts you have of hightailing it are ruined, since it's immediately obvious he's spotted you — he waves hello.

"Where's Sally?" you ask as he gets close enough to hear you.

"Oh, we had a great dinner at Umberto's up the block, but then she wanted to go home," Mike replies. "She said she had a million phone calls to make — she has to tell everybody in the universe about Flair, you know."

"I know," you say with a smile. "Sally doesn't keep news to herself — good or bad."

"I'm learning that," Mike says. "Hey, I was just going to get some ice cream. Want to join me?"

"Sure," you say. Ice cream sounds really good right now.

At the ice cream parlor at the next corner, you order your cones. Mike gets a double rocky road, and you get a single black cherry scoop. Mike pays for both cones almost absentmindedly.

As you walk out of the parlor, licking your ice cream, you realize that Mike hasn't said anything to you for a while. It's like he's with you, but not really there.

"What did you eat for dinner?" you ask, trying to warm up this sudden frostiness you're getting from him. "I love Umberto's. Did they have that awesome peach chicken special?"

"I had the lasagna," he replies.

You both sit down on a bench near the ice cream parlor, under a buzzing streetlamp. Another silence falls between you and Mike, and you rack your brain for something to say. "Um . . ." you try finally, "how's your ice cream?"

"Oh," Mike says, looking away from you down the street, "it's good."

"Mine's delicious," you say.

He doesn't reply at all.

Okay, now it's obvious something's wrong with him. Maybe he's just being distant because he's preoccupied with something, but it's rude to invite someone for ice cream and then basically ignore her!

Mike starts jiggling his foot, burning off some extra energy, you suppose. Did you do something wrong, something to offend him? You think back — everything seemed cool and comfortable until you went into the ice cream parlor.

Maybe he's disappointed at having to get ice cream with you instead of with Sally.

Maybe he's totally in love with you but just doesn't know how to say so, and the wild emotions inside him are leaving him paralyzed and speechless.

Maybe he's just really boring.

Whatever the reason, the silence between you two is driving you crazy. You have to say or do something!

If you take the plunge and admit that you've had a thing for Mike from the moment you saw him, turn to page 106. ➡

If the cold shoulder he's giving you is just too annoying to handle anymore, and you take your ice cream and go home, turn to page 142. ➡

If you demand to know why he's being so mopey, turn to page 160. ➡

♥ "I don't want to knock you when you're down," you tell Dan, "but our fullback Carlos is famous for his kick-bomb. He booted it like half the field twice in the first quarter before he surprised you. It shouldn't have been a shock."

"Ooh, right on," Mike tells you.

"Yeah," Dan says. "I was hoping nobody was going to mention that." He pops a fry into his mouth and grins way too wide at you. "Thanks."

"That's why I'm here," you say. "To keep you guys honest."

Sally giggles. "She's good at it," she says. "She always keeps me in line." Then Sally and Mike share a weird glance that you don't get. Some in-joke between them, obviously. You file away the glance to ask Sally about later.

Maybe it's time to improve the overly critical vibe at the table. "Actually," you say, "I thought all you guys were great out there. It was probably just home-field advantage that helped us kick your butts today."

"You're a tough chick to impress," Walt tells you.

"That's cool," Mike adds.

"I'm hard to impress, too!" Sally puts in, elbowing Mike in the ribs.

He rubs the spot she hit. "There's a reason why you two are best friends, right?"

Is that the reason you and Sally are best friends, because you're both hard to impress? You think Mike missed the mark on that one. Sally fell for him the moment he spoke to her, and you have to admit that he's definitely impressed you too. Well, he's impressed you *physically*, at least. He still hasn't proven that he's anything but a dumb, sexy jock.

Sally's phone rings, a simplified version of the "Hollaback Girl" melody. She checks the display. "My mom," she says with a grimace, and answers. You listen as Sally gets more and more agitated talking to her mother. The upshot of the conversation is that Sally has to go to the mall next door to help her mother safely bring home her aunt's wedding dress. You are going to be abandoned at the diner because Sally's mom drove her new electric hybrid car . . . which is only a two-seater.

"Now?" Sally whines into her phone. "Right this second? I'm here with —"

Sitting next to Sally, you can hear her mother say, "Yes, *now*," very clearly before she hangs up.

Sally throws her phone into her bag. She's rough on phones — she goes through like one a month. She makes a face at you, an annoyed frown. "I've got to —"

"I heard," you say. "You're ditching me for an ugly wedding dress."

"Mike?" Sally says.

Mike breaks away from whatever he was saying to his teammates. "What?" he asks.

Sally nods at you.

"Sally's got an errand to run," you tell him. "Can you give me a ride home?"

"You're taking off right now?" Mike asks Sally. "Like this second?"

"That's what I said," Sally replies grimly. "I've got to go." She looks at Mike for a heartbeat, and you can totally tell that she's considering whether or not she should give him a quick goodbye kiss. She probably feels too awkward with the other guys at the table, because she pushes past you out of the booth.

Sally kisses you on the cheek instead of Mike. "Be good," she tells you and winks. She waves to the rest of the table, and a minute later she's out the door.

It may sound silly, but you have a feeling that Mike having to give you a ride home alone is the mysterious hand of fate at work. It reeks of destiny.

You shouldn't have been secretly hoping that you'd get alone time with Mike. It's incredibly disloyal that you feel a twinge of happiness that Sally's left. But you just can't help how you feel.

In Mike's car a half hour later, you have no idea what to say to him. It's a nice car — an old green Jetta, very broken in and comfortable, but still solid. You stay awkwardly silent until he gets off the main strip and turns in to the wooded back roads toward your house. "Uh . . . ," you try, "you're a very steady driver."

"I don't like being hurried," Mike says. "It's one of my, um . . . indiosyncracies."

You get the feeling that he attempted that big word to try to impress you, and the fact that he messed it up is kind of endearing . . . and also just dumb. He's lucky he's so cute.

"I don't like being rushed, either," you tell him. "My parents are always trying to get me to move faster — just one of the ways they harass me. But you can move fast. . . . I saw you running on the soccer field. That was very fast."

"Yeah," he replies. "That's because I want to run, not because anyone's making me. It's totally different."

"Exactly," you say. "Like when a book is assigned to you in class, it's not nearly as interesting as one you just find on your own."

Mike is silent as he makes the next turn leading up the hill to your house. He chews on his bottom lip. "I probably should read more," he says. "I'm not a fast reader, but I like it."

"I'm a very fast reader," you say softly.

He glances at you with a quick smile on his handsome face. "I could tell you're a smarty," he says. He turns onto your block.

"Third house on the left," you tell him.

As he slows down before reaching your driveway, you find yourself wishing you could spend more time with him alone — the ride was too quick. Mike is clearly imperfect, and he's so not your usual type . . . but there's just something compelling about him that makes you want to stay near him.

"Is that bad?" you ask. "Being a smarty?"

Mike pulls up to a stop. "No," he says. "It's good."

While you're very pleased that he complimented you, you can't help feeling a little disappointed, too. You already know you're smart . . . part of you wishes he had said something nice about your looks instead. Sally has already told you that he called her pretty.

Of course, it would be so incredibly inappropriate for Mike to tell you you're pretty . . . even if he thinks it. He's Sally's boyfriend. He's just giving you a ride as a favor to her. You feel like a lousy friend for even having wished for a compliment about your appearance.

"Thanks," you say, "for the ride and everything."

"No problem," Mike says.

You open the door and climb out into your driveway.

As you shut the Jetta's door, you hear him say, "Anytime."

You smile as you walk toward your house. Mike really is sweet.

That night, Sally calls and drops a bombshell.

"I think I'm over Mike," she blurts out.

You flip over onto your stomach on your bed. "When did this happen?" you ask, trying to keep your voice calm even though your heart has suddenly begun thumping.

"It was the wedding dress," Sally says. "Am I crazy? I started thinking about how I just would never even want to marry Mike in a million years. I just couldn't picture us together like that."

You laugh. "Isn't it a bit soon to be thinking of getting married?"

"Of course," she says. "But there should at least be a remote chance, right? It shouldn't be totally impossible, or else what's the point?"

"Mike's a really nice guy," you say. "He said nice things about you when he drove me home." Which he totally didn't. He didn't even mention her. You close your eyes and lean your forehead against your big purple teddy bear named Miss Priss that Sally gave you on your thirteenth birthday.

"I think that's the problem," Sally replies. "There's a thing that can happen when guys are too nice. Your feelings for them can just stop. It's not like I'm in love with anyone else."

After you hang up, you lie on your back, hugging Miss Priss to your chest.

Sally says her feelings for Mike have stopped. That means she'll be dumping him soon.

He's not the most intelligent guy in the world . . . but he doesn't pretend to be, either. Mike was so adorable when he said that he knows you're smart.

And he's just so truly good-looking, with that all-American face that you just want to study, like its shape contains all the secrets to your happiness.

Have you started having feelings for him? *Real* feelings?

If you have to admit that yes, you do feel something for Mike, turn to page 88. ➤

If, honestly, you realize that your attraction to Mike was fleeting, turn to page 56. ➤

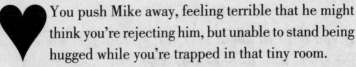You push Mike away, feeling terrible that he might think you're rejecting him, but unable to stand being hugged while you're trapped in that tiny room.

"I can't take it," you cry, your voice shuddering. "This is the worst. I don't know what to do, I can't take this! Help me!" You can barely stop yourself from screaming. "Help me!"

"Hold on," Mike tells you. "It'll be okay."

"No!" you shout, flailing your arms around in the darkness. "I've got to get out of here — now! *I've got to get out of here!*"

"Okay!" Mike says. "Okay!" He leans back and then barrels forward, slamming his shoulder against the door.

It doesn't open.

"Get me out of here!" you wail.

"I will!" Mike shouts. "Calm down!" He lifts his leg and kicks the door with all his strength, hitting it right over the lock.

The door slams open and bounces off the wall behind it. It probably would have swung closed and locked again if you hadn't instantly thrown yourself into the doorway. You scramble out into the light, gasping for breath.

"I'm sorry," you say, still shaking terribly from your claustrophobia. "I just can't take small spaces."

"It's cool," Mike says. "We're out. You're all right."

You nod. "Thank you," you say. "Oh, thank you so much for getting me out of there."

Mike pulls you into his arms again, and this time his embrace makes you feel safe.

Turn to page 190. ➡

You take a deep breath, shift on the bench so that you're facing Mike, and tap him on the shoulder to get his attention.

He raises an eyebrow at you, his eyes filled with some powerful emotion you can't identify. Mike looks like something's eating him up from the inside.

You almost give up and go home without saying anything, but you're sick of keeping these feelings for him bottled up inside you until you feel like you're going to burst.

"Yes?" he asks. When you don't answer immediately, he turns his head away from you again.

"Listen," you say. "Look at me, Mike."

He turns to face you, his lips pressed so tightly together that they're turning white.

"I know I haven't known you very long," you blurt out, "and I know you're dating my best friend, so I probably have no right to say this to you. But I can't stop thinking about you. I care about you, and I want to get to know you so much better. I don't want to hurt Sally, but I've felt this connection since the first day I met you —"

Mike closes his eyes.

You stop rambling, ashamed at how much you've

confessed, feeling more vulnerable that you've ever felt in your life.

Then Mike's eyes flutter open, and his expression is so intense you almost gasp. He reaches out and gently strokes your cheek with the side of his index finger, gazing into your eyes. "Me, too," he says. "I've been thinking all those things you said, but I was feeling so wrong about it all, how terribly I would be treating Sally if I told you how I feel . . . how *much* I feel for you. It was driving me crazy."

"I was going crazy, too," you whisper. "I feel it, too."

"I think . . . I know I've fallen in love with you. Hard," Mike admits. He runs his fingers through the hair falling around your neck, which feels wonderful.

"Yes," you say. You're amazed at how unsurprising this conversation is, like you expected to hear these exact words all along. You feel excited and joyful, but it's not the scary emotion you were expecting — it's more like the understanding that you're doing exactly what you're supposed to be doing with your life. "That feels so right. But —"

"Sally," Mike says.

"Sally," you agree. "I'm glad we told each other how we feel, but it doesn't change anything. We're still not being true to someone very close to me."

"I care about Sally, too," Mike says. "But when love is this strong, it's destiny, and we can't turn back now. Things will work out somehow. I promise."

You want so badly to believe Mike's words, to believe that you can be with him without hurting your best friend. The longing you have for Mike is so strong, it's making you dizzy, and you grip the back of the bench tightly.

It would be the perfect time to kiss him, with beautiful words of love still floating and flashing in the night air like fireflies.

If you give in to what Mike says is destiny and kiss him now, turn to page 117. ➡

If you say, "I can't do this to Sally," turn to page 127. ➡

♥ "Forget about my brother," you say. "Peter's a real team player . . . because he can't develop a personality of his own." You immediately regret dissing your brother like that — the two of you actually get along pretty well.

Mike stares up at you for a second, looking blank. "Team player," he repeats. He chuckles. "No personality of his own, yeah." He laughs again, a low rumble that doesn't make him sound very bright. "Team player," he says again, shaking his head.

"Peter has a personality," Sally says from her seat very close to Mike on the bench.

You glance at Sally sharply. She seems annoyed, her lips in a tight line. Sally only meets your eyes for a second before she looks away.

"Not that I care," she adds.

You narrow your eyes. The crush Sally had on your brother had *better* be history. Nothing ever came of it in reality, but you had to suffer through hours upon hours of Sally going into hyperdramatic mode over how it was breaking her heart that Peter barely knew she was alive. It had just been creepy trying to give Sally advice about how to snag your own brother, and you felt greatly relieved not to have to listen to her whine about him anymore when her crush just fizzled out and she got busy with the fall musical.

Unbelievably, Mike is still laughing at your joke about your brother. He's obviously not the brightest bulb on the Christmas tree. Still, you find yourself unable to hold that against him — he's just so good-looking! You're glad you didn't show him the photo, though. He doesn't seem like the type to appreciate art.

Sally tugs playfully at the corner of Mike's ear. "You think that's funny, huh."

"It was the way she said it," Mike replies, pulling away from Sally's pinch and nodding his head toward you. "Your friend's funny."

"Anytime I can harsh on my own family for your amusement," you say, "just let me know."

Mike rewards you with a smile, and something inside you softens, a sudden, dangerous stirring of emotion. Why is a genuine smile on a handsome face so powerful?

"Not that it matters, really," Mike says. "We'll get even in the playoffs next week."

"Hey," Sally says to Mike, "you think Walt would like her? I think maybe Walt would work."

Mike shrugs noncommittally, unscrews the top of a water bottle, and pours the warm leftovers out on the grass.

"Who's Walt?" you ask. "I don't know if I like where this is headed."

"Cute guy on Mike's team," Sally says. "The one with the blond floppy hair?" She turns to scan the soccer field, but quickly turns around again. "Gone."

"He went to the diner," Mike offers. "Where we're going."

"He's just your type," Sally tells you. "I think you're his type, too. Mike won't mind if you come with us. Right, Mike?" She nudges him and he shrugs again, and then Sally faces you. "Come with."

"My type, huh?" you repeat, mulling over the offer. You have a vague recollection of a reasonably cute blond guy who kept having to push his long, sweaty hair behind his ears while he was hanging back on defense. Your basic impression of him was of tallness, skinniness, and paleness. Which, yeah, you've been known to crush on willowy guys before, especially if they're smart.

But why do you get the feeling that you might have a new type . . . dark, compact, and athletic with insanely beautiful blue eyes and maybe a little less brain, for instance? Of course, that type will be at the diner, too. . . .

"Yeah, okay," you decide. "I'll come."

The diner near the mall is a big roadside chrome palace, and it's as busy as ever, filled with all kinds of people from around town, with more than a few tables of Clearview and North Cliff kids. Mike charges right into the diner, heading toward a round corner booth where four Eagles in their blue uniforms are having burger feasts. You and Sally hurry after Mike and slide into the booth after him.

You recognize the guy across from you as Walt — he looks better now that his hair is dry. Already deep into their postmortem of the game, the soccer jocks don't really stop their conversation when you arrive. Walt just turns to include Mike in what he's saying. "We lost it in the passing game," Walt continues. "If there's any chance that Jamie thinks he's going to score, he won't let go of the ball, even if he's triple-teamed."

"We just got tired," Mike argues immediately. "Did you see Lyon out there? He's got great moves, but he's so out of shape — he was like huffing and puffing before halftime."

Why can't you stop looking at Mike's bicep as he leans forward on the table? It's just an *arm*, really, isn't it? You see guys' arms every day . . . why are you so mesmerized by Mike's? He scratches his nose and even that light flexing bunches up the whole bicep, pulling his sleeve taut.

Mike orders a burger, exactly matching his teammates' meals. Sally gets an Oriental chicken salad with mandarin oranges and the dressing on the side. You're just in the mood for a basket of fries and a Diet Coke.

"And you, Dan, man," Mike says, pointing a pickle at the shorter, freckly guy on his right, "what was up with you today? What, were you just daydreaming out there?"

Dan just snorts a little and shakes his head. "Do you

want to talk about *your* great play? Peter on the Stallions blew right by you."

You wince, flashing on the frozen image you caught in your camera.

Mike clenches his jaw and pokes at a piece of lettuce on his plate.

"She's Peter's sister," Sally pipes up, and all the boys turn to stare at you. "But we were both rooting for you guys today."

"Speak for yourself," you tell Sally with a smile.

"Ooh," Walt says. "We're fraternizing with the enemy."

You laugh and reach for the ketchup as the guys go back to their soccer chatter.

Sally leans really close to your ear. "Aren't soccer players adorable?" she whispers. Then she sits back and gets a dreamy expression on her face while staring out the window.

Odd. For some reason, you got the feeling that she wasn't necessarily talking about Mike.

"Yeah," you reply. "They are."

Then you try to focus on what the guys are talking about.

"I wasn't daydreaming," Dan continues, "but how are you supposed to react when defense gets off a whopper of a kick like that? How could I have seen that coming?"

"By staying alert," Packer answers.

Mike nods. "Packer's got a point."

If you join in the soccer conversation, turn to page 97. ➡️

If you suddenly realize how boring jock talk is — and jocks, too! — turn to page 39. ➡️

You jump off the picnic table and dive right into a somersault on the grass. Instantly you remember how free you felt as a little girl tumbling on a lawn, and you laugh as you unfold flat on your back, looking up at the sky.

Mike peers down at you, blocking out the sun. "Come on," he urges, holding out his hand to you. "Don't just lie there."

You let him help you up, and then you both get busy tumbling around the sunny park. You try a handstand and fall onto your back, but then you roll around on the grass for a while before pulling yourself up to do a couple of cartwheels in a row. You can't remember the last time you had this much pure, innocent fun.

Mike pulls himself up into another handstand, and you sit back and watch as his shirt falls down over his face, and you can see the taut ripples of his stomach muscles as he struggles to keep his legs up in the air. He's so incredibly hot.

He falls over, and lies where he landed, laughing. You crawl over to him and lounge beside him. "It feels so great to be so . . . physical," you say. "I usually spend so much time just using my brain."

Mike turns toward you and grins wickedly. "I'm so glad I could help you get back in touch with your body," he says.

You reach out to smack him for being fresh, but he grabs your wrist and pulls you toward him. You land face to face, and it's the most natural thing in the world to kiss him.

Major sparks flash and sizzle all around you . . . and all throughout your body. Mike is an amazing kisser, so gentle, but so passionate. With your eyes closed, you're totally lost in the perfect moment.

"Oh, Sally," Mike whispers. "That feels so good."

Uh. . . .

Abruptly, you pull away from him and sit up. Mike immediately reaches for you again — he doesn't even seem to have realized that he just called you by your best friend's name. All the pleasure you were feeling has now curdled inside you. He was obviously thinking about Sally the whole time.

"What's the matter?" Mike asks. "C'mon back here."

He is so clueless. Should you tell him what he said?

If you think, Why bother? and just go home, turn to page 142. ➡

If you think his calling you Sally is too rude to get away with, and you tell him off angrily, turn to page 146. ➡

Mike leans closer to you, and the loving expression on his gorgeous face makes you feel soft inside. You half expect to hear birds singing around you, or the music of joyful angels celebrating your true love. You close your eyes with a sigh, and wait for fireworks as his lips touch yours.

His lips feel funny. Squishy, somehow.

It doesn't feel very nice.

Huh. No fireworks. Not even a sparkler. What a let-down.

He gets your whole chin goopy. You've gotten gentler kisses from your dog.

You break off and breathe into his neck for a moment, trying to get rid of the nasty flavor in your mouth by swallowing repeatedly. You're feeling terrible about the whole kiss — not only because of what it would do to Sally if she found out, but because it was bad. Awful. The worst kiss you've ever had. But how are you going to tell him that after your big declaration of love?

You suddenly can't imagine what you ever saw in Mike.

"No!" you hear someone scream.

You turn to look toward the ice cream parlor. Sally is

standing in the rectangle of light from the parlor doorway with a look of complete horror on her face.

She saw you kissing Mike.

You blink at her as her expression goes from total shock to heartbreak — you can see the moment when her heart shatters as she realizes she was betrayed by both her best friend and her boyfriend. Tears spurt out of her eyes, trailing quickly down her face. Then she spins around and barrels away from you down the dark sidewalk, wailing as she runs.

You give Mike a shove to get him off you, and you race after Sally.

"Sally, wait!" you scream. "It was an accident. Don't run away! Let me explain! I didn't even like it!" You chase her for another block before she starts to slow down. "It was a bad kiss!"

Sally wheels around to glare at you, her face red with rage. "It doesn't matter if it's bad or good!" Sally hollers at you. "Is that really supposed to make me feel *better*? You kissed my boyfriend, and you ruined everything. You betrayed me! My best friend betrayed me! How am I supposed to kiss him now? How am I supposed to trust you ever again?"

You break down into tears, too. "I'm so sorry," you sob. "I didn't even enjoy it. I'm so, so sorry."

"I don't think we can be friends after this," Sally says. "I would *never* have done that to you." She runs away again, sobbing. The sounds of her choking cries are like needles poking into the center of your chest.

You stand there in front of a children's clothing store on the cute shopping street, but the world has never looked uglier to you. Hot tears roll down your face, and you slump down onto the stoop outside the store's entrance, weeping in complete misery.

You have just lost your best friend.

All because of a guy with the most putrid and rancid breath ever.

The End.

♥ That night, you slip with relief into a hot bubble bath and relax, letting yourself let go of all the stress you've been carrying about Mike and Sally.

He's a pretty boy, nobody's denying that, least of all you. But that doesn't mean he's right for you or Sally. Just because someone is good-looking does not mean he's a good person.

Why is that so obvious and yet so easy to forget?

The more you think about Mike, the more you realize you totally don't like him anymore. He's a jerk, plain and simple.

It was wrong of him to flirt with you when he's supposed to be dating your best friend!

As the hot tub soothes away your tensions, you solemnly swear to yourself, cross your heart and hope to die, that you'll be a good friend to Sally from now on.

Your first task? Working with her to improve her awful taste in guys. Definitely.

Sally's so easily blinded by a cute face, beautiful eyes, and a nice butt.

She's sort of stupid that way.

The End.

120

♥ At 7:30 that night, Sally shows up at your front door to pick you up for the party. You look over her shoulder and see Mike waiting in his green car in front of your house.

Sally's wearing a cute, tight yellow sundress and a light denim jacket. "You look great," you tell her, and she checks out your dark jeans and your favorite pretty blue top with the low-scooped, embroidered neck.

"Good," she tells you.

"Midnight!" your dad yells from somewhere else in the house. "Preferably *before* midnight!"

You verify this with Sally. "Yeah, okay, no problem!" you holler back at your father, and the two of you go down the walkway to Mike's car.

Of course he's got a cool ride. It's some kind of old car that's as lean and sporty as Mike himself. It could use a new paint job. You have to squeeze into the backseat and sit sideways to fit.

You can barely see Mike in the driver's seat, but just knowing you're in his car makes you smile to yourself. Also, the whole car smells like him — a good, clean boy smell that you inhale deeply and savor.

Darren's house is tucked into a high hillside and

surrounded by forest. It's big, with odd, jutting angles, and it looks like it was built from redwoods. The winding drive up the hill through the woods has been quiet and dark, but the house is blazing with light and blaring music.

A wave of noisy excitement hits you in the face when Darren lets you in. Darren's most notable feature is the stupid tricornered pirate's hat he's wearing. Behind him, and down the hall, you can see about twenty North Cliff guys laughing, bumping each other, stuffing their faces with chips, and dancing with a few girls in the living room. There are maybe four girls dancing, and another group of three standing in the hall near a bathroom. They seem okay, but not like anyone you're dying to meet.

There are no adults in the house, just a bunch of juniors and seniors all hyped up, having a great time.

Mike leads Sally and you deeper into the house, into a gigantic kitchen with black cabinets and stainless steel surfaces everywhere. It looks like the food prep area in a fancy restaurant. There are six guys in the corner, laughing uproariously at something they're up to by the drinks counter in the corner.

"Darren's mom's a chef or something," Mike explains.

"Nice," Sally says. She sounds a bit nervous, and you feel a flash of sympathy. It's got to be rough to be at a party where a lot of strangers know her new boyfriend better than she does. You give her hand a reassuring squeeze, and she squeezes back gratefully.

The guys in the corner spot Mike, and they all cheer and call him over.

Mike introduces Sally and you. The guys' names are Scott, Spencer, Rob, Walt, Ron, and Jazz. Jazz is cute, and Walt kind of is, too, but the other four are generically jocky. They're pouring "suicides" at the drinks counter, mixing all the sodas together and daring each other to drink the concoctions.

"It's Walt's turn," Ron announces, and he hands Walt a cup filled with some yellowish, fizzy cola mixture. Walt sips tentatively.

Right in your ear, Sally whispers, "Walt's the cute one," and you nod. He does seem cuter to you now, with curly blond hair and really clear skin. You decide that Mike isn't the only guy in the room worth getting to know better.

"It's not bad," Walt decides.

"Let me try," you say, jumping right in.

"Woo!" Jazz exclaims. "A brave lady!"

You smile at him as you take the cup from Walt. Everybody watches as you take a sip.

It really isn't too bad — just painfully sweet, with a flavor a little like prune juice. You drink the whole cup, which gets you a big cheer.

Sally pushes up to the counter. "That was just all soda, right?" she asks Walt.

He nods.

"That's too easy," Sally says. "You guys are amateurs. I'll mix something none of you will touch."

"She's a mad scientist!" Spencer shouts, and then he laughs in a really dorky Transylvanian accent.

"Go on," Mike tells Sally, "do it." He sounds surprisingly serious. "I can drink anything you can invent."

"So can I," you add.

"Ooh," Rob says. "A challenge."

"You're on," Sally says. "Both of you!" Then she's all business at the drink counter, clearly relishing having all the guys pay attention to her every move. She pours some cola in a plastic cup, and then looks around for other liquids. She finds a little coffee sitting in the carafe of a coffee maker. "How old is this?" she asks.

Nobody knows — Darren isn't in the kitchen. By the film of grease floating on the coffee surface, you figure it's at least a day old. Uh-oh, that won't taste so good.

Sally adds some of that to her suicide cup. Then she opens the door to the big metal refrigerator and peers around inside.

"Mustard!" Spencer suggests.

"No," Jazz says. "Milk."

"Good idea," Sally tells him. She adds a dollop of half-and-half. "Anything else?" She searches on the top shelf of the fridge. "Aha," she says. "Pickles. Pickle juice."

Your stomach flip-flops. Mike looks a bit worried, and the other guys whoop in approval.

Sally adds a big stream of neon green pickle juice to her nasty mixture. The cream instantly curdles, floating in white chunks and bits, and the whole mess turns a sickly greenish brown. She swirls the mixture, and then pours half into another cup. "Here you go," she says, handing you one cup and Mike the other.

"Wait a second," Walt says. "Hold up both cups next to each other." Mike and you comply, and Walt leans over to inspect them. "Okay," he decides. "They look even. I just wanted to make sure."

Sally arches her eyebrows at Walt, but she says nothing to him. "Are you ready?" she asks you and Mike.

You can smell it — sour, like old garbage.

"Whoever drinks the most wins," Spencer explains. "If you both drink it all, then it's a tie."

"And then Sally has to drink the next batch," adds Jazz. "If neither of you finishes, Sally doesn't have to be part of the next suicide if she doesn't want to."

"Let's do it," Mike says. He already sounds queasy, which makes your stomach lurch.

Everyone falls completely silent as you and Mike stare at each other grimly while slowly raising the cups to your lips.

You know it would be foolish to drink the noxious sludge. It's probably poison. At best, it's going to taste wretched.

But Mike is staring right at you with his gorgeous, high-voltage blue eyes, and suddenly you'd really like to beat him in Sally's challenge — and to hold your own in front of Sally. It would feel so satisfying to take them both down a notch.

"Together," Mike says.

If you pour that horrible gunk into the sink, turn to page 28. ➡

If you chug it, turn to page 226. ➡

"I can't," you tell Mike. "I just can't do this to Sally. You and I can't start a relationship based on betraying someone close to us. That's such an awful way to start — our love would be doomed from the beginning."

Mike nods, biting his lower lip, and looking so sad that you're moved to hug him tightly. He feels strong and muscular in your embrace, and the sadness of having to let go almost overwhelms you. You force yourself to pull away from him, already missing what you're sure is the last hug you'll ever give him.

"You're right," Mike says. "You're right, but I hate it. Now that I know I love you, I can't still go out with Sally —"

"Maybe you can," you interrupt. "Maybe with me out of the picture, you'll see how much she means to you."

"I just don't feel for her the way I feel about you," Mike says firmly. "How can I go back to her now that I know what real love feels like?"

"You're breaking my heart," you tell him, getting misty-eyed. "Stop it. It's not fair to say these things to me, when you *know* what we have to do. I love you, I do, but I won't be able to love myself if I break Sally's heart. I'd rather break my own heart than hers."

Mike sniffles. "Why does heartbreak always sound so

127

corny?" he asks. "It's like there's totally no way to be sad about love and still be cool."

You laugh, and then feel even sadder — how many laughs will you miss out sharing with Mike because of what must be done?

"I'm going to break up with her anyway," Mike says. "What else am I supposed to do?"

"That's between the two of you," you reply. "Leave me out of it — it's the only way to be fair."

Mike bows his head, and you can feel him trying to come up with another argument to make you stay, to find the magic words that will make your love possible. But you've thought of everything, and there's just no way it will work.

"Remember when I showed you that picture of you I took?" you ask.

"Of course," he says sullenly. "It was just a couple of days ago."

It feels like a lifetime. "Well, you told me that you wanted to see the picture because you could handle the truth," you remind him. "We need to face the truth here, too. The truth is we can't be together, and we need to accept that."

"You make it sound so easy," Mike complains.

"No, it's terrible," you assure him. "I'm going to do nothing but cry for weeks, I promise you."

You both sit quietly on the bench for a long moment, until Mike reaches out and takes your hand. "I don't want to lose you," he says.

"I've got to go," you say. If you have to be the strong one, so be it. You pull your hand away from Mike and stand up.

"No," he says. "What if, after I break up with Sally, a couple of months later when everything calms down and she's moved on . . . maybe then you and I can give us a try?"

"Maybe," you say sadly. "You never know what will happen."

With that, you turn around and walk slowly toward home. Saying no to Mike was the hardest thing you've ever had to do, but you know from the pure, righteous feeling glowing inside you that you've done exactly the right thing.

Turn to page 135. ➡

♥ "Okay," you tell Sally. "You really want to sneak out and meet him?"

She nods her head vigorously. "Absolutely," she says. "And you have to come with me, please."

"Fine," you say, giving up. "I guess I can't let you face your scary boyfriend all alone."

"Great!" Sally chirps. "Get dressed!"

Sally's plan is to meet Mike at a nearby playground halfway between his house and hers. Once you and she have made it safely outside, you actually start looking forward to this adventure. It's a beautiful, warm night, with a bright crescent moon, and everything is vibrating with a feeling of anticipation. You also have to admit that you're pretty excited about seeing Mike again. . . .

You and Sally get to the playground before Mike, so you play on the swings while you wait, swinging as high as you can and then bumping the plastic strip seats into each other so that you wobble out of control for a moment.

When Mike arrives, you and Sally are all worked up and giggling, but you stop laughing when he says "Hey" to Sally but ignores you one hundred percent, as though you don't even exist.

"Come with me," he says to Sally in a husky voice, and

she smiles and follows him over to the wooden jungle gym where they can sit together. Within seconds, they're making out like crazed rabbits.

This is exactly what you didn't want to happen. Ugh, how long are you going to have to sit there, listening to them sucking face? This is ridiculous, and really, so gross. What are you supposed to do while they're getting busy?

You wish you'd brought your MP3 player with you.

With a big sigh, you move over to the slide and sit at the bottom. It's actually pretty comfortable to lie back against the slide with your feet out in the sand below, the whole metal length supporting your body. You lie there looking up at the stars, listening to Mike and Sally kissing. It's boring, annoying, and icky, but at least you're helping out your best friend, and the sky is lovely to stare up at.

All those stars . . .

You must have fallen asleep, because you wake up and it's dawn and you're covered in dew.

The sound of kissing has stopped. You sit up and peer around in the darkness. Mike and Sally are gone.

You stand up, and a little note on a gum wrapper falls into the sand. You snatch it up and read it.

It's in Sally's handwriting: "Call me!"

You stumble home alone.

Turn to page 120. ➡

♥ "I can't just leave Sally here like this," you tell him. "This afternoon you were acting like you were dating her, and now you just want to leave her lying alone on a golf course?"

"Whatever," Mike says. "It's not like she's going to freeze to death or anything. It's like seventy degrees."

"That's not the point," you reply. "Let me at least wake her up and talk to her, tell her where I'm going."

"You're coming with me?" he asks, trying to sound nonchalant.

"Maybe," you answer. You have to admit, just the idea of sleeping on a beach with him makes your heart pound in a way you're pretty sure you're not ready to handle.

"Decide quick," he tells you. "Hanging out here is getting old fast."

You kneel down next to Sally and put your hand on her arm. "Sal," you whisper. "Wake up, it's me."

"Uh . . ." she murmurs groggily.

"C'mon, wake up," you say. "I can't leave you here. Can you get home by yourself?"

"What happened?" she whimpers.

"You're okay," you tell her. "You barfed from the bad yogurt and then fell asleep for a while."

"Uh," she says again. "Oh, the taste in my mouth . . ."

You don't even want to imagine what the aftertaste of yogurt barf is like. "Sally," you say, "can you get home by yourself? It isn't far."

"No," she moans. "No, don't leave me."

"She'll be fine," Mike says.

You stand up and glare at him with your hands on your hips. "No, she won't," you tell him. "I'm not going to abandon my best friend, and if you can't respect that, you should just get lost now. I've got to take her home."

Mike laughs. "Girls," he says. "You're all the same."

"I'll bet we are," you reply. "To a pig like you, that is."

He gives you a nasty look that quickly turns aloof and haughty. Then without another word, he zooms off on his motorcycle, buzzing quickly off the greens, onto the road, and out of sight.

You heave a deep sigh, and then settle down next to Sally to wait for her to recover enough for you to help her home.

How could you even have considered going with him? A loser like that is going nowhere, and he's just going to bring everyone down with him.

For a fleeting instant, you can't help wondering if you could have tamed his wild ways, changing him for the better. You quickly shake your head to clear it. *I will not think about Mike any more*, you vow.

It has nothing to do with the fact that he scares you.

Not at all.

In your later life, during quiet, lonely moments, you will sometimes remember this night, and you'll think of Mike longingly as the hot bad boy you let get away.

The End.

The next day, you turn off your cellphone, hole up in the newspaper's darkroom, and throw yourself into your photography, trying to forget all about Mike. There's nothing like keeping yourself busy with something you love to do to distract you from your miserable love life.

You've been in the darkroom for maybe an hour when you hear someone calling you from the newspaper office.

"Hello?" you hear Mike's voice calling. "Are you in here?"

You push your way out of the darkroom and blink in the bright lights of the office. Mike has a gigantic grin on his face.

"What?" you ask. "What are you doing here? I thought we decided not to —"

"I've got amazing news," Mike says. "Are you ready for this?"

"As ready as I'll ever be," you reply. "What's going on?"

"It's unbelievable," he says, hopping up onto a waist-high flat-file cabinet and swinging his legs excitedly. "Sally called me this morning and broke up with me on the phone."

You take a step closer to Mike. "You want to run that one by me again?"

"*She* broke up with *me!*" Mike hoots. "It's all because of you — because of your photograph at the show. That Flair agency called Sally last night and offered her a gig in Paris, which is apparently just the beginning of a long-term modeling contract as the face of some new perfume. She's leaving right away, like this weekend, and since she didn't want a long-distance relationship, she hoped I'd understand if she and I broke up while she was away."

You stand in the middle of *The Clear View* office, trying to process all this astounding new information. "I shouldn't have turned my cell phone off," you mutter to yourself. You feel a little dizzy, and wobble a bit on your feet.

"Maybe you should sit down," Mike suggests.

"Yeah," you say, and you sit down on the floor.

Your best friend is leaving for Paris immediately. You're going to miss her so much, but you couldn't wish for anything better for her. This is what she's always wanted, and now she's getting the chance to follow her dream. It's truly incredible. And it's because of the picture you took of her!

Maybe you'll even get to visit her in Paris!

You just sit there and shake your head in amazement.

"You know what this means, don't you?" Mike asks.

"Uh . . ." you reply, "free perfume?"

He laughs — a happy sound that you were afraid you'd never hear again. "No," he says. "It means there's a new truth about us that we have to handle. For the first time, nothing stands in our way."

You climb to your feet. "I can handle it. We'll have to wait until she's gone before we go public," you say.

"Absolutely," Mike agrees. "And we should wait until Sally's settled in Paris before springing it on her."

"Yeah," you say, taking a step toward where Mike is sitting. "We don't want to freak her out, but I have a feeling with all those French male models around her, she's not going to worry about us at all."

Mike opens his arms wide. "Come here," he whispers, and you rush into his arms, pressing your face against his warm chest.

"Wow," you say, feeling awed about how life can turn in directions you never would expect. You couldn't have chosen such a perfect outcome if you'd tried.

Mike puts his hand under your chin and tilts your face up toward him. "Flair and Paris got the model," he says softly, "but I got the beautiful girl."

You kiss him. Tingles buzz throughout your body, and you give yourself up utterly into his embrace.

The End.

♥ You've always wanted to ride on a motorcycle — now's your chance. Mike puts on his helmet and hands you one, too. He helps you climb on behind him.

"Put your arms around my waist," he tells you, "and hold on tight."

"Yes, sir," you say, and you slide your hands around his torso. You have no trouble holding on tightly.

The bike vibrates as Mike drives across the fields. It feels so fast! You bounce over ridges on the landscape, shifting closer to Mike every time you land. Ten minutes into the ride and you've got your entire weight leaning against his back, snugly fitting against his lean contours.

Everything on the golf course looks weird and mysterious in the moonlight, and at high speed the trees pass by in gray blurs. You turn your head as you whip past mysterious thickets of bushes that look like the entryway to a haunted forest.

Mike pulls up to a stop beside the golf course's water trap — a sizable pond. With the engine idling, you can hear the buzz of insects and the eerie, surprising *gunk!* sound of the frogs.

"You've been friends with Sally a long time, right?" he asks you.

"Since third grade," you answer. "We've been best friends that whole time."

Mike nods. "Is she always so . . . clingy?"

"No . . ." you answer carefully. "She's not clingy at all."

He laughs at that. "Oh, man, that girl is suffocating me, and only after a week. Like, she's just desperate to know how I'm *feeling* about her, every second of the day."

"So what do you want?" you snap at him. "A girlfriend who just leaves you alone, lets you do your thing?"

He flips up his visor and looks at you sharply. "Yeah," he says. "Anything wrong with that?"

His eyes are such a beautiful color in the moonlight that you forget for a second that you're really pissed off at him for the things he said about Sally. "Uh . . ." you say.

"It's like she expects this fairytale romance thing," Mike continues. "That . . . that just seems so corny. I'm just not into that."

"Maybe when the right girl comes along," you say softly, "you will be."

Mike snorts in laughter. "I seriously doubt it," he replies. "I don't have time for girls, anyway. I'm saving up to get out of this boring town. I might not even wait until I graduate. It's just so . . . small and stifling around here."

"It seems okay to me," you say. You had always thought

you liked your town, but now that he mentions it, it is a small place, and nothing exciting ever happens. "It is pretty slow, I guess."

"The understatement of the century," Mike says. He flips his visor closed. "Let's go back," he tells you, and you hold onto him tightly, but then loosen up a little, wondering if the way you're holding him could be interpreted as *clingy*.

The ride back isn't as much fun and seems to take a lot longer, the wind picking at your whipping clothing like pinching fingers.

When you stop at the meeting point, where Sally is still out of it, you slide off the bike and hand the helmet back to Mike.

"Thanks for the ride," you tell him. "It was fun." At least the way to the pond was fun, before he started being so negative.

"It doesn't need to be over yet," Mike says. "I feel like doing something *wild*," he says, getting excited, "like staying out all night, sleeping on the beach!"

He nods his head at you. "You should come with me," he tells you. "That would be cool." Mike smiles at you a little, and for the first time since you've met him, he seems sort of vulnerable, and you can see the scared boy behind the tough guy act.

Which, of course, makes him even more attractive.

You don't know. He really was a jerk about Sally . . . and about girls in general. This is not someone you should get

140

involved with at all. You're a good girl, and you like your safe, predictable life . . . right?

Besides, Sally is still passed out at your feet — and regardless of how Mike labels their relationship, Sally definitely considers Mike hers. On the other hand, Sally is the one who dragged you here against your will in the first place, when you weren't even feeling that great. She hasn't exactly been looking out for *your* best interests.

"So are you coming or what?" Mike wants to know.

If you tell him that you have to talk to Sally about it first, turn to page 132. ➤

If there's no way you'd ever stay out all night with him and you tell him exactly what he can do with his sleazy offer, turn to page 144. ➤

Lying in bed that night, you give in to the sadness that you've been trying to deny ever since you got home. You turn on your side and hug your old teddy bear as you wonder if you ever really had a shadow of a chance with Mike.

As painful as it is to admit, you have to face the facts — Mike isn't all that.

Most important, though, he isn't worth risking your friendship with Sally over. There were so many moments during the past few days when you really stretched the boundaries of what Sally might consider betrayal, and as you think back on the mistakes you made, you shake your head against your pillow, wondering how you could have been so stupid to push your luck so far.

You will be a better friend to Sally from now on. There's no way a guy will ever come between you again. You absolutely swear it.

Really, you only feel sad about losing the *idea* of Mike — losing the thought that someone out there was into you. If you're being realistic, you know there will be better guys for you in your future.

You wouldn't want to date a guy who cheats so easily on

his girlfriend anyway! How could you trust him to be faithful to *you*?

You flip over onto your back, staring up at the grayness above you, watching the light from a passing car headlight shift in soft angles across the ceiling. Sally really shouldn't be dating such a player, either, you decide.

You'll have to tell her the truth. Soon.

It may hurt her at first, but your friendship is strong, and she would expect you to tell her what's really going on. You didn't do anything with Mike that's so bad she can't forgive you . . . especially since he's the one who was chasing after you.

Now that you've decided to tell Sally about Mike's cheating ways, your sadness lifts, and you feel rather pleased about dropping out of the game.

Maybe you're just not ready for a boyfriend, or maybe you just haven't met the right guy yet.

You're okay with that, really.

For now.

The End.

♥ "Oh, please," you tell Mike. "I'm so over your tired bad boy act." You know you have to be rude to him — it's the only language guys like him understand.

Mike shrugs again. "Suit yourself," he says. "It doesn't matter to me."

"Yeah, nothing matters to you, does it?" you accuse him. "My best friend is lying right there. She's supposed to be your girlfriend, so why are you coming on to me?"

Mike snorts. "Don't flatter yourself," he says. "I wasn't coming on to you. I was just being friendly, but forget it now."

"Don't you care that Sally's sick? She's your girlfriend."

"She's not really my girlfriend," Mike says. "I don't have girlfriends. No girl's going to tie me down. None of you are worth it."

You stomp away from him, back toward Sally. "Buzz off, motorcycle boy," you snap. "You don't impress me."

"Smell ya later," he calls back. Then he revs up his bike and zooms away.

When your anger fades and you can see straight again, you help Sally to her feet.

"Where's Mike?" she asks groggily.

You throw her arm around your shoulder, supporting her weight. "He had to go," you grunt. "He's such a jerk, Sal."

She puts her head on your shoulder. "Oh, I know," she tells you. "I'm just seeing him to freak out my mom."

You smile as you help her toward the road, pleased that both of you are done with Mike for good.

Sally yawns. "Yeah," she says. "All I had to do was smell him to know he's a loser. One whiff and I puked, right?"

"Right you are," you say. "Guys should not make you puke."

You both giggle at that the whole way home.

The End.

♥ "You just called me Sally!" you tell Mike. "That's so *astoundingly* rude. Why would you do that?"

"I did what?" Mike replies. "I called you Sally? When?"

"Just now!" you shoot back. "While you were kissing me."

Mike's face flushes for a moment, but then he sits up and shrugs. "Well," he says finally, "she *is* my girlfriend. So it's really not that surprising. I guess I must really love her, or something."

"Then why were you making out with me?" you demand to know.

"Well, you're pretty," Mike says. He reaches out a hand toward you, but you slap it away, and he glares at you. "Maybe I wanted to see how it felt, that's all."

"And?"

He shrugs again. "And it was okay. I'm really not that into you. Kissing you just confirmed that for me."

You close your eyes for a moment, absorbing this awful information. This afternoon has taken a terrible turn, and you wish you could do anything to turn it back the way it was.

You climb to your feet and brush grass off your pants. Mike has made you feel so skeevy that you want to rush home and take a shower. At least his grossness makes it easier for you to play it cool. "Yeah," you lie, "even before you called me Sally, I knew I wasn't really into you, either. You're just not my type."

Without even looking back at him, you stride to the parking lot and drive yourself away from the park, and away from Mike.

You don't make it three blocks away before you have to pull over and cry for a while before you recover enough to drive yourself all the way home.

If you know that someday you'll have to tell Sally the truth about what happened with Mike, turn to page 142. ➡

If you know you'll take your secret about what you did with Mike to the grave, turn to page 153. ➡

♥ "I'm just not feeling well enough," you tell her. "Either go without me, or cancel."

"No," Sally says. "Uh-uh. Go make yourself puke if you have to, but I am not missing this meeting with Mike, and I'm not going alone. I'll play the big card if I have to."

You close your eyes and sigh. She's got you. "Fine," you say. "Don't get crazy. I'll come."

The "big card," as she calls it, would be to tell everyone you know that when you were eleven years old, you stole a pair of tighty-whitey underwear out of Steven Ohlmeyer's gym bag and took them home. You can only plead that you were crushing on him insanely at the time. It was really your first crush, and you were totally nuts over him, but that doesn't really excuse that you slept with his undies beneath your pillow for a whole week until your mom found them and made you throw them out.

You don't know what you were thinking. A month later, you couldn't even stand to hear Steven's name.

Snuggling his underwear was not your best moment. Yes, you were out of your mind. But is Sally going to black-mail you with that for the rest of your life?

Sally calls Mike on his cell, and she arranges for the two of you to meet him at the golf course in twenty minutes.

You've both sneaked out to the golf course before. It's easy to break into — there aren't any fences around the greens — and it's empty and quiet at night.

The fresh air helps settle your stomach, and by the time you reach the golf course, you're actually glad you came — especially when you see Mike. He's leaning on a motorcycle, and he looks devastatingly hot.

Sally starts running over to Mike, but when she gets a whiff of the motorcycle exhaust fumes, she stops and grabs her stomach. "Ooh, that smell," she says, and she turns around and tosses her yogurt cookies into a giant fern.

Funny, you feel fine now.

Sally sinks to the grass and puts her head down. "Bad," she says. "Just need to rest." Then she curls up with her head on her arm and closes her eyes.

Mike raises his eyebrows at you, amused at Sally's illness. He gestures for you to come closer.

Warily, you step toward him. There is something . . . magnetic about him, you have to admit. Part of it is how well his jeans fit over his legs, and part of it is the way he seems to hold himself aloof from everything around him, like he's always bored and nothing will ever excite him again.

You know you could excite him.

Which is such a crazy thing to think.

"Typical," he whispers to you, waving his hand at Sally. "It's always something with her. Really, I'm just about done with it."

"Don't tell me," you say. "It's so not my business, and I don't want to know."

He shrugs. "Well," he says, throwing a leg over his motorcycle seat and holding the bike upright, "we're here. You want a ride?"

As if. His supposed girlfriend, and your supposed best friend, is lying right there on the grass. Yeah, she's pretty out of it, but doesn't he have any decency at all?

Mike revs the motor, and you feel it vibrate and thrum all throughout your body . . . and you're not even on the bike yet.

If you decide that you'd be crazy to get on Mike's bike, but realize he's too hot to resist and so you climb aboard — turn to page 138 ➡️

If you tell him to get lost, turn to page 144. ➡️

♥ "Let's just go in there and grab him," you suggest to Mike. "Between the two of us, we should be able to handle a little kitty."

Mike shakes his head, unsure. "Damien is a monster," he says.

"Oh, come on," you say. You grab Mike's hand and pull him toward the storage closet.

The closet goes deeper than you expected, and it's really dark back there. The light from the hall is just enough for you to make out the shadowy outlines of the objects around you. You don't see any sign of Damien. All you see are bags of pet food and kitty litter, with the occasional broken cat transporter thrown in a pile.

"This is a bad idea," Mike says.

"Are you afraid of the dark?" you tease. You step further into the closet, deeper into the darkness.

"No," Mike says, sounding a little nervous. With a deep sigh, he follows you in. "Okay, now what?" he asks.

"When we spot him, we grab him," you say. "We've got to be quick —"

In a gray blur, Damien zips between your legs and zooms out of the storage room like a shot.

Mike and you start laughing. "Well, that worked!" Mike gasps.

"He's out of the storage room, isn't he?" you snap back, still laughing.

Mike's laughter trails off, like he's just thought of something terribly serious. He takes a step toward you. "You're so much fun to be with," he says in a husky voice. "You make me laugh, and that's so hard to find."

"You make me laugh, too," you whisper.

You suddenly realize how close he's standing to you, in a dark closet. There's a delicious tension so thick between you that you feel like you could grab it and twist it like taffy.

Mike shifts, and now he's even closer. Your hand brushes against his arm, and the feel of his fine arm hair makes your fingertips tingle.

That's when the door swings shut with a click, closing you in darkness.

Turn to page 199. ➡

On Monday morning, you spot Sally in the hallway at school and hurry over to her. You've secretly resolved never to jeopardize your friendship again, now that you've put that whole mess with Mike behind you. "Did you study for the history test?" you ask breathlessly. "I totally forgot last night, and now I'm going to flunk it —"

You get a look at the expression on her face, and you cut your words off dead. Sally looks beyond angry. She looks like she just doesn't care about you at all anymore, like you're dirt on her shoe.

"*Skank*," she hisses at you. Then she turns around crisply and marches away, leaving you shocked in the hallway. You hear applause, and you glance around to see some girls you know clapping their approval at what Sally just said to you. You back away slowly, your face flushing, and then you rush over to your locker.

A girl named Maryann is pulling books out of the locker next to yours. You share some classes with Maryann, but really, you barely know her. She raises her eyebrows at you while you fumble nervously with your combination lock.

"Nice going," Maryann says dryly. "I can't believe you even dared to show your face here today."

"What's going on?" you ask her. "Do you know what this is about?"

Maryann shrugs and balances her textbooks under her arm. "All I know is what I've heard," she says. "Sally's boyfriend told her that you stalked him and tried to kiss him, and now Sally hates you and she's spreading it to the whole world."

You look down the hallway, and your stomach tightens when you see that everyone is staring at you with disgusted looks on their faces, rolling their eyes and whispering to each other.

"That didn't happen," you whisper to Maryann. "That's not what happened."

Maryann slams her locker shut. "Save it for somebody who cares," she tells you, and then she pushes her way down the hall.

Slumping back against your locker, the full, enormous horror of what's going on hits you, and you close your eyes, hoping it will all go away.

You have become a total outcast.

No one will ever believe you if you try to defend yourself . . . especially since the truth is that you're not all that innocent.

You've lost your best friend. You've lost *all* your friends. You can hear their nasty whispers echoing off the hallway walls.

And you're struck with the sudden understanding that you probably deserve everything that you're getting.

Well, that pretty much finishes you socially at Clearview High. You might as well go join the burnouts in the parking lot, because your life as you knew it is over.

The End.

"Tell him your mom woke up and caught you," you suggest. "Tell him not tonight. It's too late, and he'll see you tomorrow."

"Tomorrow's forever from now," Sally argues.

"You know you're being irrational," you shoot back. "Stay here with me. We'll watch a movie."

"That's lame," Sally says, but you can tell she's softening.

Your stomach clenches suddenly, and a wave of nausea wriggles up from your stomach. "You're not feeling that well," you remind her. "You said so yourself."

Sally lets out a long, huffy breath. "Fine," she says through gritted teeth. "I'll tell Mike I'll meet him tomorrow. But if he breaks up with me because of this, you'll owe me so big."

"He's not going to break up with you."

She makes one last-ditch effort to convince you. "Oh, *pleeeease?*" she begs, batting her eyelashes and trying to look cute.

"Stop," you say. "I'm not a guy. You can't trick me with flirting."

"Okay, okay."

An hour or so into the movie, your stomach is really in knots. It feels like there's a twisted hard lump like a gnarled apple stuck in there. You glance over at Sally. She's sitting up against a giant pillow with her hands holding her stomach.

She presses pause. "Do you want any ginger ale?" she asks. "I want some. I think it will settle my stomach. It does that, right?"

"I think so," you say. "Because of the bubbles. That sounds great. With ice, please."

While she's getting that, you take deep breaths, wondering when this wave of sickness is going to pass. It feels really gross, and it's making you sweat. You *hate* sweating. It always makes you break out.

You're so glad you and Sally didn't sneak out to meet Mike. It would be totally mortifying for him to see you like this.

Sally comes back in, sipping from one glass and holding out another to you.

You take the ginger ale and drink quickly, wanting the bubbles to do their magic.

"I don't think it's working," Sally says. She's standing alongside her bed, weaving on her feet. She puts the glass down on her side table. "No, I'm pretty sure it's a lot worse." She gags, a disgusting prebarf. "Oh, no," Sally moans, and she runs into her bathroom and closes the door behind her.

You put your ginger ale down, too, because here it comes — you are going to yack, there's no doubt about it. Especially now that Sally's making nasty retching noises you can hear right through the door.

You rap on the door, "Let me in!" you beg.

"I'm okay!" she calls back. "I'm okay, I'll be out in a minute."

Your time is almost up. Sally's only trash bin is a wicker basket near her desk — you can't puke in that. The other bathroom upstairs is between her older brother's room and her parents' room. You'll totally wake them up if you go in there to barf, and you don't think you could handle that embarrassment.

Outside, then, you think wildly. *I've got to get outside!*

You run down the stairs just as you hear the toilet flush upstairs. It's too late to turn back now, though — you fling open the front door and stumble onto the lawn. A motion-sensitive spotlight clicks on, flooding the grass so that it looks greenish black. You're almost too far gone to care that anyone in the neighborhood could see you spew. Nature has taken over.

You turn around and stumble toward the bushes along the edge of the house. Maybe you can make it there, where at least you can vomit and maybe nobody will notice.

A rippling heave wracks your body.

That bad yogurt needs to come out.

Now.

Sally is standing in the doorway of her house. She's

wearing a white robe and holding on to the side of the door-frame.

"What are you doing here?" she asks.

Throwing up, you think, before you realize she's not talking to you.

Turn to page 188. ➡

"Mike?" you ask tentatively. "Will you tell me what's going on with you, please? You're putting out waves of misery that I could sense from across the street."

Shockingly, Mike leans back into the bench, covers his face with the hand not holding his ice cream cone, and starts blubbering into his fingers. It only takes a second before he's turned into a sobbing mess.

You put your hand on his knee. "What is it?" you whisper. "C'mon, you can tell me."

"Sally told me something, right before I ran into you," he blurts out wetly. "It's all over between us. Her news isn't just about Flair — while we were at dinner, she found out that the Flair people showed that photo you took of her to some perfume company . . . and she's already got a modeling contract!" Mike leans forward, breaking down into sobs again.

Not knowing what else to do, you rub his back. "Isn't that good news?" you ask. "Shouldn't you be happy that she —"

"No!" Mike screeches miserably. "You don't understand. The contract is with a perfume company in Paris! France! She's leaving right away, and she's going to be gone for six months!"

160

•

You pull away from Mike a little. You can't believe Sally didn't call you on her cell the second she heard. You're supposed to be her best friend! "It's only for six months," you say. "You guys could still make it work."

Mike wipes his eyes, and you take a good look at him. His face is all puffy and he's got a trail of snot coming out of one nostril. You can't believe you ever thought he was attractive.

"This whole separation coming up just made me realize how much I love her," Mike says with a deep sigh. "When I think about how close I came to messing that up by flirting with you . . ." He starts tearing up again.

Whatever. You're fine with you and him going nowhere. Really. After all his gooey romantic talk and now this sobbing declaration of love for Sally, you realize he's much too much of a wuss for you anyway.

You pat Mike on the head and leave him alone to sob out his love to the lamppost as you walk home, thoughtfully licking your ice cream.

Sally is moving to Paris, huh. It kind of surprises you to realize that you won't miss her that much. Honestly, you're relieved she's going away — you've been living in her shadow too long, dealing with all her over-the-top drama, always having to tell her how beautiful she is every second of the day. Frankly, it was exhausting.

And now you won't have to compete against her for sub-par, wimpy guys like Mike!

You finish your black cherry cone and lick your lips as you stand on the sidewalk in front of your house.

It seems like everything's working out for the best.

The End.

"No," you tell Mike firmly. "I can't, and that's that. I really won't have a good time if you force me to go."

He gives up with a shrug, and when you catch the look of relief on Sally's face, you know you've made the right choice. You understand how early relationships are like baby birds — helpless, defenseless creatures, tiny and peeping sweetly and unable yet to fly. You don't want to be the one who crushes Sally's baby bird.

A couple of hours later, you get a call from Sally. "I hate my mother," she fumes. She sounds furious. "This time, I really hate her."

"What?" you ask. "Did she nix that white dress?"

"No, this is so much worse," Sally replies. "Like a *thousand* times worse. When Mike drove me home, nobody was here, so he came in . . . and so he came up to my room, okay?"

"Uh-oh," you say.

"Yeah," Sally says. "I mean, we were just kissing. Totally just kissing. I can't believe I didn't hear her car. I always hear her car. So then she acts like Mike being in my room is like the worst crime ever."

"Did her head explode?" you ask.

"She totally lost it," Sally replies. "So now I'm grounded, of course, when I have an awesome party to go to. Get this — she says I need time to *cool off*. It's so not fair."

"I figured that's what was coming," you say. "That sucks."

"Yeah," Sally says. "But it's still Friday, and I'm not just moping around here. Want to sleep over?"

You accept.

After a night of painting your toenails and sitting around listening to Sally make indignant phone calls to all your other friends explaining her imprisonment, the story changing slightly with each retelling, you and she take a break to raid the refrigerator.

"I'm not letting any junk food in the house," Sally informs you. "It's health, health, health for me."

"Don't you miss taste, taste, taste?" you ask.

"Every minute of every day," Sally replies. She pulls out a pint container of plain yogurt. "I opened this a couple of days ago, but it should still be okay," she says. "We can add blueberries to it."

It doesn't taste quite right going down, but between the two of you, you finish the container.

"Sally?" her mother calls down the stairs. "Your father and I are going to bed."

Like I care, she mouths silently at you, and you giggle.

"Don't stay up too late, okay?"

"I won't, Mother," Sally snarks back.

You watch TV in Sally's room for a while, but there's nothing really good on, not even any funny infomercials or shopping shows. You're starting to feel oddly hot, and your stomach is flipping alarmingly. You take deep breaths to settle yourself down.

Sally is squirming uncomfortably next to you on her bed. Finally, she sits up and clicks off the TV. "I'm so bored," she says. "Let's see if Mike's home yet."

She checks her instant messenger and there he is on her buddy list. They quickly make a plan to sneak out and meet each other.

"Get dressed," she tells you. "You've got to come with me."

"Nah," you tell her. "I'll stay here and cover for you. You didn't want me to hang out with you and Mike when you thought you were going to the party, remember?"

"This is totally different," Sally says. "That was a party at a house with lots of people. My parents would have known where I was. I don't meet guys alone at night. You're coming with me."

"Oh, Sal," you say. "I'm really not feeling that great. I think it was the yogurt. Can't I stay here this time?"

She tugs on your hand. "C'mon," she says. "I don't feel that well either, but you don't see me complaining. It'll be fun."

If you feel too sick to sneak out with Sally, turn to page 148. ➡️

If you try to convince Sally to stay in and watch a movie with you, turn to page 156. ➡️

If you go along with Sally's plan to sneak out, turn to page 130. ➡️

"I'd love to see the office," you say. "I could even help you walk the dogs. If that's not against the rules."

"Really? You want to come with me?" Mike asks, as if he hadn't been fishing for you to assume his invitation the whole time.

You smirk at him. "I just said I wanted to come, didn't I?" You gesture around at the bare-bones and purely functional office of *The Clear View*. "It's got to be more exciting than this place."

"Cool," he says. "You showed me your pictures, and now there's something special at the vet's office I want to show you."

"What?" you ask.

Mike pulls out his car keys, jangles them in front of you, and gives you a devilish smile. "You're just going to have to wait and see."

You love Mike's car. The battered leather interior of his old BMW is as smooth as butter against your arms, and the whole vehicle feels elderly, hearty, and kindly, like a grandfather on wheels.

Mike turns on his music, and you smile when you recognize the latest song by your favorite band.

167

"Turn it up," you tell him, and as he drives through the streets of your town, you both whisper-sing the lyrics together. During a cool drum solo, Mike pretends to be a headbanger for a second, which cracks you up. This melodic song is a world away from any kind of headbanging heavy metal.

Something's tickling your arm, so you rub the spot, and you pull away a long, red-blond hair that was stuck to the seat. Sally's, obviously. You quickly drop the hair, but not before you feel a twinge of guilt about being in Mike's car without her there.

Maybe Sally wouldn't mind. It's a good thing that you're getting to know her boyfriend better, right? Maybe she'd even be happy that you and he are becoming friends.

Yeah . . . that might be true if you weren't so into him.

You glance over at Mike. He's paying attention to the road, and you decide that you like the way he drives — steadily and carefully, but not too slow, either. His profile, tight with concentration, is ridiculously perfect. His cheek-bone and nose are set at angles that complement each other just right, and his black eyebrow has an arch in it that echoes those angles. His chin is a little pointy from the side, but it's softened by the fullness of his lips, which are almost too pretty.

And so kissable.

"Sally must love visiting the vet's office," you say, trying to force your brain to behave itself. "She's been obsessed with bulldogs for her entire life. But she can't get one, because her mother says she doesn't want slobber all over their house."

"They are really slobbery," Mike agrees. "But I don't know if Sally likes this office. I haven't taken her here yet."

As he pulls into a small office park, you wonder if it's completely awful of you to feel pleased that you're getting to know a part of Mike's life before Sally does.

Actually, it *is* completely awful of you, and you should be ashamed of yourself.

But since you're already here. . . .

Inside the office, the space is kind of small and cramped with filing cabinets and a wall of leashes and collars for sale. It smells kind of musky. Down a hall, you can see a couple of exam rooms, and part of an X-ray machine in another room. As soon as Mike shuts the front door behind you, the sound of a bunch of dogs barking issues from someplace you can't see.

"They're in the basement," Mike says. "They're only alone for a couple hours in the early evening — a technician comes on for the last shift and stays all night. So that's why I need to stop by to check on them. Want to go down and meet them?"

"Totally," you reply. "That's why I'm here."

If that was really the only reason you were there, you wouldn't keep picturing the stricken expression on Sally's face if she ever found out you went there with Mike without her.

Down in the basement, a surprisingly large room holds two separate dog areas surrounded by chain-link fences — one for big dogs, and one for the small guys. They all start to howl the second you and Mike step into sight.

"It's okay, guys," Mike shushes them, moving his hands in a keep-it-down gesture. "It's okay, chill out. Relax. It's okay."

You're quite impressed with the way the dogs listen to him — some still whimper and fidget, but most of them settle down completely. Mike's voice was very soothing when he was calming them.

You like guys who like dogs. Guys who like dogs are usually not afraid to show affection, and they understand responsibility better, too. Mike climbs up another notch in your esteem.

Why are you keeping track of the notches in your esteem anyway? This is *Sally's* boyfriend, you remind yourself, not yours.

After a few minutes of hanging out with the dogs, Mike says, "I told you I had something special to show you."

"Yeah," you say. "You did."

"Come with me," Mike says, and he leads you over to a door on the other side of the room, out of view of the dogs.

Inside are cats in small wire cages. A few start purring or meowing when you enter, but most of them just peer at you and Mike suspiciously with glowing eyes.

"I love cats," you say. "I've got two — Mabel and Gladys. They hang out with me all the time."

"Yeah, cats are cool," Mike says. "But check this out." He stands in front of the cage at the end of the row and waves you over.

In the last cage are six tiny gray kittens. "Ahhh," you breathe. "Cuteness to the millionth power." The kittens have sleek bodies but roundish, puffy heads, and they would sort of look like lions if they weren't so tiny and didn't have such pretty bright blue eyes. Maybe lions have blue eyes, too . . . you'll have to look it up on the Internet when you get home.

"Want to hold them?" Mike asks. "It's good if people handle them often."

"Absolutely," you say, and you reach your hands out for a kitten.

Mike scoops up a sleepy one and gently plops her into your hands. She stretches and yawns, and then curls up right in your hands, going back to sleep. You pet her head gently while Mike pulls another kitten out of the cage.

This one is wide awake, and Mike holds him up against his shoulder. His kitten starts purring so loudly that you can hear him from where you're standing. He bumps his head against Mike's chin on purpose, which is just totally adorable. Mike and the kitten together are so insanely cute that they should be illegal.

As Mike opens the cage again to put his kitty back in, another kitten leaps out and skitters across the concrete floor. "Aw," Mike complains. "That's Damien. He's always escaping, and he's fierce and really hard to catch. Give me a hand?"

You nod and pass the sleepy kitty back to Mike. Then you take slow steps toward Damien, making clicking noises at him. He scoots under a chair and glares at you, his ears back flat against his head.

"Careful," Mike warns as you reach out for Damien. "He's just a kitten, but his claws are sharp."

Damien hisses at you, and you pull your hands back quickly. The kitten zooms out from under the chair, bounces off a wall, and then zips into a dark storage room.

Almost immediately, you hear yowling and shredding noises coming from inside.

"We've got to get him out of there," Mike says. "It sounds like he's ripping up the cage liners. Uh . . . unfortunately, the mitts we usually use to catch mean cats are in the storage room. The light bulb's burned out in there, too. Any ideas?"

"Yeah," you say. "Leave it to me."

If you squat down in the storage room doorway and shake a cat toy, trying to lure Damien out, turn to page 177. ▶

If you bravely enter the dark storage room to grab Damien, turn to page 151. ▶

If you forget the kitten and kiss Mike instead because he's so sweet and cute, turn to page 182. ▶

♥ You lean down toward Mike's face in your lap, and he raises his head at the same time. There's an awkward moment of repositioning your noses — right or left? — but then you work it out and you're kissing.

Oh, you didn't know a kiss could feel like this. The sensation of his lips against yours vibrates in to you, tingling down your spine, jangling with pleasure.

Without breaking away, he twists his body so he can hold himself up better, turning so you're kneeling side by side. He cups your face in both his hands as he kisses you softly over and over again.

There is no doubt in your mind that you and Mike are meant to be together. You're absolutely sure you and he are going to be together a long time, that your love will last, and everyone in school will —

Out of the corner of your eye, you catch a glimpse of red hair in the doorway.

Sally's standing in the hall, staring into the bathroom with a look of total shock on her face. The surprise changes to rage in a flash.

"Get off him!" she hollers at you, stepping into the

bathroom and pulling you away from Mike. She's stronger than you expected.

You fall backward against the plumbing under the sink. The pipes dig painfully into your back.

"What's been going on up here?" Sally yells at you. She glares at her boyfriend, who wipes his mouth with the back of his hand. "Mike, what are you doing with her?"

"I'm the one who helped him —" you begin.

"I wasn't talking to you," Sally says hotly. "Save it."

"But —"

"I said I wasn't talking to you!" Sally screams, her face bright red, veins popping out in her neck.

"You were laughing at me," Mike says. "I got sick."

"That's your own stupid fault," she tells him, pushing her hair back on the sides, trying to calm herself down. "I was laughing because it was funny. That's the game, to make each other barf. You lost. Get over yourself."

"He was sick," you say defensively, "and you laughed at him."

"Please," she shoots back. "He got sick because he drank something foolish. And anyway, how does me laughing at my boyfriend during a game suddenly give you permission to mack on him?"

You have no good reply to that, and suddenly you feel entirely sorry.

"Yeah, I thought so," Sally says. "That's what I thought."

She starts to sniffle, and she turns away from you, her face crumpling with tears. "How could you do this?" she says wetly, taking deep breaths to pull herself together. "You're my best friend."

"I'm still your best friend," you say softly.

"No," Sally says, shaking her head, wiping her eyes dry. "You *were* my best friend. But now you're dead to me."

You start to cry. "Sally, don't throw away years of friendship —"

"You can't throw away something that's already in the trash," Sally tells you, and she walks out the bathroom door. "Come on, Mike," she says.

"Mike," you say, pleading.

He gets up and follows her into the hall. Mike only glances back once and gives you a shrug. Then he disappears around the corner with Sally.

That shrug breaks your heart.

You never meant anything to him, really. That's so obvious now. Maybe he was kissing you to make Sally jealous, or maybe he was just giving you a pity kiss because you helped him, but he couldn't have cared about you, or he would have stayed.

Oh, why didn't he stay?

The crushing feeling in your chest is so painful. Your heart squeezes, clenches, and you sob on the bathroom rug.

You don't even have a best friend anymore.

You hate yourself for betraying her, and that hurts so much worse than anything else.

It's the kind of pain that lasts forever.

The End.

You crouch in the doorway and shake a bell-and-feather toy. "Here, kitty, kitty," you chirp. Damien makes another scary hissing noise from inside the closet.

You turn around to look at Mike. "Wow," you say, "he's really worked up —"

"Watch out!" Mike shouts.

You glance back at the doorway just in time to see a little ball of gray fur leaping toward you. Teeth and claws zoom right at your face.

With a scream, you fall backward just as Damien hits your chest and scratches you hard, grabbing the toy out of your hand. You land in a puddle . . . of something.

Damien bounces away, scrambling up a chair to leap onto a big bag of cat food on a shelf. The bag rips, and a stream of dry cat food shoots out at you. Before you can even blink, you're covered in kitty kibble.

You struggle to your feet, brushing the food off you. Your whole butt is wet from the puddle you landed in. "What is that stuff, anyway?" you ask Mike.

"Uh . . ." he says. "Cat pee. Can't you smell it?"

Now you can — and it's one of the worst smells in the world.

"That's why we have a drain in the floor," Mike says sheepishly, "to make cleanup easier."

You stare down at yourself in shock. Damien has pulled threads out of your shirt, you've got cat food bits all over you, you screamed like a little girl in front of Mike . . . and worst of all, *you fell in cat pee.*

If you freak out from pure embarrassment and get really upset, turn to page 190. ▶

If you shrug off the grossness and bravely continue trying to capture the kitten, turn to page 186. ▶

♥ "Sorry," you say. "Good luck with everything."

Halfway down the stairs, you hear the sounds of the party, and you feel like a heavy weight has just been lifted from your shoulders. You didn't realize until now how much Mike's arrogant, judgmental attitude has been stressing you out all day.

Now you just don't care. It's as if he barfed out all the coolness into the toilet. You so don't need his bad energy in your life.

Sally sees you and rushes over and grabs your hand when you reach the bottom of the stairs and the greenish marble in the entryway. "Is he okay?" she asks.

"Yeah," you reply, "he's fine. Listen, Sal, about Mike, I don't think you should . . . maybe you should think about —"

"I'm done with him," she interrupts. "How sick was it that he actually thought it would impress us if he drank that nastiness I whipped up? I don't know what I was thinking, being all into him."

You beam at her, and give her a hug. "I'm so relieved to hear you say that," you tell her. "It would be so awful if you loved him and I didn't even like him. What would we —"

"Let's not think about it," Sally says, giving you a squeeze. "Let's go dance."

179

"Perfect," you say with a smile.

You and Sally push through the dancers until you're next to Walt, Rob, and Jazz. When they see you coming, they turn away from the North Cliff girls and shuffle closer to you and Sally.

The song switches. "I love this one," you say, and you get into the groove, and Sally's right there with you. The two of you have even practiced dancing together to this song in your room.

Halfway through, Jazz steps into the middle of your routine, facing you. Over his shoulder, you see Sally grin at you right before she turns to face Walt.

You boogie with Jazz for a while . . . and he's good. Not afraid to move his hips or try some fancy moves every now and then. And he's totally responding to you, like you're dancing with each other as a form of intense, wordless communication.

When the song changes, you smile at Jazz, and he smiles back. He has the most amazingly straight, white teeth, which are so nice they almost make you feel self-conscious about your own smile.

"You're a good dancer," you tell Jazz.

He laughs and blushes, pleased but modest. "Not as good as you," he says.

"You're not seeing anybody, are you?" you ask him bluntly, amazed at your own forwardness. It just seems totally normal to ask.

Jazz doesn't seem to mind the personal question. "Nope," he says, swaying to the music. "I'm free as a bird."

"That's exactly the right answer," you say, stepping forward to dance closer to him. "That's good."

The End.

That kitten isn't going anywhere for a while, so you face Mike. He looks at you, surprised at the expression on your face.

"You," you say, "here with all these animals. It's more than cute, more than adorable . . . you're really getting to me." Then you close the distance between you and Mike and kiss him right on the lips.

Mike holds you a little way away from his body. "Where is this coming from?" he asks. "I wasn't expecting this —"

"I've felt it from the beginning," you reply, "and I know you feel it, too."

Mike stares into your eyes for a long moment, considering. His eyes flutter with concentration. Then his face relaxes, and he pulls you toward him and kisses you like you always dreamed you'd someday be kissed.

You break away from Mike when Damien starts making yowling noises from the storage closet.

"Um . . ." Mike says, licking his bottom lip, "I really should get Damien back in his cage."

"Yeah," you say, closing your eyes to savor the feelings his kiss created inside you. "It's not good to leave him loose like that."

"I know what to do," Mike says. He opens a cupboard

where a couple of little cans of tuna fish are stored. "For cat emergencies," he explains. As soon as he pops the tuna lid, all the cats in the room start meowing greedily, and a tiny, puffy gray face with bright blue eyes peers around the entrance to the storage room.

"Want some tuna, Damien?" Mike whispers in his soothing voice. "C'mon, kitty, kitty. If you want tuna, you're going to have to come and get it."

Damien takes a step out of the closet, but then freezes and darts back in again.

Mike dumps the tuna out on the floor, and Damien can't resist — he's on that tuna like a shot. After a few moments allowing the kitten to chomp away, Mike reaches out and strokes Damien's back gently. The kitten doesn't flinch — he's too busy eating.

Carefully, Mike scoops up Damien and the rest of the tuna in both hands and carries him back to his cage.

"You're great at that," you tell Mike as he washes his hands. "You're going to be a great vet someday."

"Thanks," Mike says. "I know."

You both laugh at that, and you feel a sudden rush of bravery — you want to see Mike again, so why not invite him out? "Hey," you say in a normal, casual tone of voice, "do you want to come bowling with me tomorrow night? I'm not that great a bowler, but I still think it's fun."

"Sure," Mike says. "I haven't been bowling in ages." He frowns. "But what about Sally?"

"What *about* Sally?" you shoot back. You know that makes you sound terrible, but you're feeling bold . . . and you tell yourself that Sally has such rapid boyfriend turnover that she probably won't even notice that you've stolen Mike.

"What should we do about her? I can't take you out if I'm supposed to be her boyfriend, can I?"

"No," you say, "you can't. You'll just have to break up with her first. I can't go out with you until you end it. It's the only proper thing to do."

You know you should feel horribly guilty for pushing Mike to break up with Sally, but whatever — you've already kissed him. It's not like that's any better. If the damage is already done, you might as well make the most of it.

"I even have a coupon for a free game at Kingpin," you say, to keep him from dwelling too much on how he's going to break up with Sally. You don't really want to know, as long as he does it. "Let's go tomorrow night."

"I'm not sure —" Mike begins to protest.

"Hey, Mike," you interrupt. "You're going to have to choose between us eventually, right? I'd rather you decided sooner rather than later."

"Uh . . . do I have to?" Mike asks with a deep sigh. He closes his eyes for a moment. "I'm not sure how I . . . I'm not sure. I don't want to hurt anyone's feelings."

"Well, you can't date us both," you reply firmly.

"I know," Mike says, biting his lower lip. "You're right. But do I really have to decide right now?"

184

If you decide to let Mike off the hook — for now — and agree to meet him tomorrow at Kingpin Lanes, go to page 83. ➡️

If you tell Mike that you'd love it if he came bowling with you, but he has to decide between you and Sally first, turn to page 197. ➡️

♥ "This is so gross!" you say with a laugh. "You really know how to show a girl a good time."

Mike laughs, too. "I'd better take you home," he says. "We'll have to put something down on my car seat, though — once you get that smell in a car, it never leaves."

"First I'm going to catch that kitten," you swear, "if it's the last thing I do!"

"It just might be," Mike jokes. "That's a devil kitty."

"Now it's personal," you say. You glance around and spot Damien backed up into a corner of the room, trying to hide. Spreading your arms so that he won't take off to either side, you slowly approach the kitten step by step, keeping your eyes focused on his little blue ones the whole time.

Damien hisses at you, but this time you don't flinch. You just continue your slow approach, staring him down.

As you get within grabbing range, Damien stops hissing and starts making an unnerving high-pitched whine. The poor thing sounds terrified.

You don't let your sympathy get in the way of your task, though. You slowly bend your knees, getting even closer to Damien. You start to reach out your hand toward the kitten, never taking your eyes off his for a second.

"Careful," Mike whispers.

Your hand flashes out and grabs Damien by the scruff of the neck, hoisting him into the air.

Damien goes completely limp, almost like he's relieved to be caught and now can finally relax.

Mike opens the cage door, and you maneuver Damien inside, drop him, and quickly close the cage.

Then you turn and smile at Mike.

"That was awesome," he says. "You totally stared him down."

You still feel stirred up inside — excited and brave, like there's no problem in your life too big to handle. You gaze deep into Mike's eyes, and both of you become serious.

"I want to see you again," you say firmly. "Meet me at Kingpin Lanes tomorrow night, 7 P.M. Now would you please take me home so I can get this smell off me?"

Turn to page 83. ➡

♥ With a horrible, raw cough, you puke a disgusting, chunky mixture of sweet and fizzy wetness. At first, it feels so wretched that you don't even care that your spew just soaked the sneakers of someone right in front of you. You upchucked a lot of gunk. It shines in the spotlight.

"I can't believe you just did that," Mike says.

You glance up. He's standing right in front of you. His were the sneaks you puked on.

Sally's laughing, and Mike shakes off his shoe, swearing softly. "That is so not cool." He doesn't think it's funny at all — he's pissed off.

It finally hits you. You just yacked on Mike's sneakers. He backs off, totally revolted.

Everyone's going to hear about this.

You climb to your feet and stare at Sally laughing, and at Mike entirely grossed out, trying to scrape his sneaker clean with a stick.

There's only one thing to do in this situation.

Flee.

You take off toward home, your throat raw from the barf, your cheeks hot with humiliation. Halfway across the lawn, tears start rolling down your face.

It's going to be a long time before you get over the mortification enough to show your face.

In the meantime, you don't ever want to see Mike again.

The End.

♥ Mike holds you in his arms, but you're still having trouble maintaining control over how upset you feel. You feel totally embarrassed that you're freaking out, which only makes your panicky feeling worse. Your heart won't stop thumping, your face gets sweaty, and you start to tremble.

"Hey, hey," Mike whispers, in the same voice he used to calm the dogs. "It's okay. You'll be okay." He holds your shoulders and looks you right in the eyes. His blue eyes are so beautiful, especially with his dark hair and tan skin. Staring into his eyes and listening to his voice helps slow down your breathing, but you're still shivering with the last tremors of your panic attack.

Mike smiles at you reassuringly. "Would it help if I invited you out with me tomorrow for something special?" he asks. "Like . . . dinner on the beach? I know a great place we could go."

Relief washes through you, and you instantly stop trembling. "Yeah?" you ask. "Yeah, it helps."

"So it's a date, then?" Mike asks.

He sounds so confident in your reply that you pause for a moment, considering. Yes, you feel safe in his arms, yes, you love how he acts with animals, and yes, he's totally beautiful . . . but you can't forget about Sally.

Mike is supposed to be dating your best friend.

And yet he just asked you out. That's just too weird . . . isn't it?

You take a deep breath. The date he's suggesting sounds perfect, but how can you do this to Sally?

"Sally doesn't need to know about it," Mike suggests, reading your mind. That's how in sync the two of you are already — he knows exactly what you're thinking.

You flinch. What does it say about Mike that he's willing to see both of you at the same time? It just wouldn't be fair to Sally — or to you — to accept his offer.

On the other hand, a restaurant on the beach sounds so romantic. Like Mike said, Sally doesn't ever need to know.

If you tell Mike that he needs to choose between you and Sally first, and that he should take you home now until he makes a final decision, turn to page 197. ➤

If you tell Mike that you'd love to go with him to a beachside restaurant tomorrow night, turn to page 228. ➤

This is wrong, sitting in a bathroom with your best friend's boyfriend reclining in your lap. Your powerful urge to kiss him is even more wrong.

You cover his eyes with your hand, cutting off the connection. Then you slap him very lightly on the cheek and shake your legs.

Mike raises his head, and you climb to your feet. "We shouldn't," you say.

"Kiss me," he demands.

"No," you reply firmly. "No, not like this."

"Because of her?" Mike asks. He sits up.

"Of course," you say. "Why else?"

"You want this," Mike tells you. "You know you do."

"That's not the point," you say. You step around Mike, and cross into the hallway before turning to look back at him. "Yeah, okay . . . I . . . I like you."

He smiles and shuffles on his knees closer to you.

You step backward. "No," you say, your voice whining a little. "I don't want to be that girl who steals her best friend's boyfriend. I don't want that to be me."

Mike stares up at you, looking puzzled and surprised.

"You shouldn't want that to be you, either," you tell

him. And then you turn and hurry downstairs, leaving him on his knees.

He doesn't call out for you, or follow.

You find Sally in the living room, on the dance floor. She's totally into it, boogying next to the three girls who were blocking the bathroom all night, near Walt, Spencer, and Rob. You slide into the room, avoiding elbows, and tap Sally on the shoulder.

"There you are!" Sally squeals, grabbing your hand and squeezing it. Still dancing, she pulls you close. "Isn't Walt cute?" she asks into your ear.

"You've got a great boyfriend upstairs who needs your help," you remind her. "I've got to go now, okay? I'm just not in the mood for a party anymore."

"Did something happen?" she asks, still bobbing to the song.

"Nothing really," you reply. "Mike barfing just kind of grossed me out."

She will never know about your sacrifice for her, and that is how it should be.

"That's pretty nasty," Sally agrees. "You're going to walk home?"

"Yeah," you say. "It's not that far, and it's a nice night. It's just down the hill."

Sally nods, and kisses you on the cheek. "Call me tomorrow," she says, and then she goes back to dancing with Walt, Rob, Spencer, and the other girls.

When you shut the door to the mansion behind you and stand on the stoop, a heavy wave of sadness hits you, and you can feel yourself wilt a little. It was really hard saying goodbye to Mike. But you know you did the right thing.

Beyond the circle of light from the house, the road downhill through the forest is dark . . . very dark.

You sigh and start walking down the long driveway, past the parked cars.

Near the end of the line is Mike's sports car. You drag your finger along the pinstripe on the side. You only got one ride in his cool car, and that strikes you as incredibly sad.

The front door to the mansion opens, and you look up.

Mike steps out onto the porch steps, lit by the bright electric lanterns on either side of the door. He shades his eyes and peers out into the darkness.

You wave to him.

He smiles, jumps down the stairs, and runs across the lawn toward you. "Oh, good," he says, panting from the run. "You didn't get too far."

"No," you say carefully. "I didn't get too far. What's up?"

Mike calms his breathing and opens his car door. "Get in," he orders you. "Let's talk."

"No," you say. "I told you. I'm going home."

"Don't," he says, holding out his hand. "C'mon, get in."

"No," you repeat, folding your arms across your chest, although really, you'd love nothing more than to sit in his car, talking to him for hours. "Quit trying to boss me around, okay?"

Mike sighs and stares into his car for a long moment. When he glances back at you for a second, you catch a surprising stricken expression in his eyes. "After you . . . helped me, and then left, I came downstairs. I couldn't find you, but then I spotted Sally on the dance floor, in the corner. She was totally making out with Walt. What a good friend *he* turned out to be. I didn't even say goodbye."

You stare at him, processing this news. Somehow, you're not surprised. Sally is like that — you've seen it before.

Mike smiles at you. His cheekbones are so gorgeous when he smiles, and he gets the cutest wrinkles on the bridge of his nose. You nod and climb into his car, dragging yourself over the driver's bucket seat to get to the passenger's side.

Mike sits in the driver's seat, leans his head back against the headrest, then turns to look at you. "What's happening with Sally," he says. "What's happened. I'm not like this usually. I take dating very seriously."

"Me, too," you say.

"I think if you're going to see somebody, you shouldn't do it casually," he explains. "There's no reason to be in it if you're not going to give your best."

You shift closer to him in your seat, pulling a leg up under you. "And this means?"

"I want to see you again," Mike says. "You're seeing me again."

"Wait —"

Mike abruptly leans forward and presses his mouth against yours. You flinch, startled, but when it sinks in that he's kissing you, you kiss him back. His lips are even softer than you expected, and you never dreamed that he would kiss so intensely, so tenderly.

The force of the connection in the kiss is breathtaking, and you have to break away to gulp air.

"Oh," is all you can think of to say.

"You're seeing me again," Mike whispers.

"Okay," you say. "Yes."

The End.

After you give Mike the ultimatum that you won't see him unless he officially breaks up with Sally, you can barely think about anything else.

As you reorganize your sock drawer, you wonder how long it's going to take Mike to come to his decision. You're not sure you can take it if the wait's really long. You smile ruefully as you arrange your shoes by color on the floor of your closet — if he doesn't make up his mind soon, at least your room will be impeccably organized.

While you're updating all the MP3 song tags on your computer, adding genre and mood settings, the doorbell rings.

"I've got it!" you screech as you clatter down the stairs. Before you open the door, you take a deep breath to compose yourself. This is the moment of truth.

And there he is. Mike. With his adorable face and amazing body. The guy you've felt more interested in getting to know than any guy you've ever met. Why couldn't he have been single? Why couldn't he *not be dating your best friend*?

"Hi," you say. "How are you?"

"I'm okay," he says nervously.

You wonder if his nervousness is a good or bad sign. "You want to come in?" you ask, holding the door open further.

"No, that's okay," Mike says.

Your stomach drops. That's definitely a bad sign.

"So . . ." you ask, "you made your decision?"

"Yeah," he says, looking down at his sneakers. "And I'm sorry . . . I can't break up with Sally. I don't want to break up with her."

Your mind reels with fragments of possible phrases, one of which must be the correct combination of words to say to make him change his mind.

Mike looks into your eyes. "It was a really hard decision," he says, "but I choose Sally."

"Okay," you say, feeling completely numb inside. "Thanks for letting me know."

You shut the door gently, and then walk back up to your room and crawl under your big comforter.

It takes you about three days to get back out of bed.

After all that, you and Sally are never really the same. She starts hanging out more and more with Mike, and you avoid her more and more. She and Mike date for the whole school year, but you don't know what happens after that, because you've lost track of her by then.

It's not sad, really. You get over Mike. Mostly.

And you love your new circle of friends — the other girls that work on the newspaper with you. Really, they're great.

None of them have boyfriends.

The End.

You try to turn the doorknob, but it won't move. It's locked. From the outside. You shake the doorknob violently, trying to get it to open.

"Chill," Mike says. "It's kind of cool that we're trapped in here together."

The word *trapped* echoes horribly in your head, and you feel the first fluttering of panic in your chest.

"I don't like small spaces," you say, your voice quavering. "I hate being *trapped* in small spaces."

Mike moves closer to you, while you fight the urge to kick the door as hard as you can, trying to break it down. "We'll be fine," he says.

"No, we *won't*," you reply. "We're trapped in here!"

Mike wraps his strong arms around you and holds you close. You can feel yourself trembling against his chest as he strokes your hair.

If you relax in his arms, turn to page 203.

If the hug just makes your claustrophobia worse and you REALLY start to freak out, turn to page 104.

199

As ordered, you gently stroke Mike's soft, straight black hair, brushing it off his forehead, tucking it behind his ear, running your fingers through the thick part above the nape of his neck. His hair feels amazing tickling through your fingers.

Mike sighs happily, and snuggles in a little deeper against your leg.

"I'm sorry you got sick," you whisper, without stopping petting his head.

"Thanks," he replies.

You swallow. "In a way, though," you say as casually as you can, "I'm sort of glad it happened. Because sitting here with you . . . like this . . . is really nice."

Mike is silent for a long moment while you hold your breath. "Yeah," he says finally. "It is."

That reply gives you the courage to forge ahead.

"Cool," you say, your mouth dry. "There was this . . . after the game today, when we met, I felt this connection between us. *Something*. Do you know what I'm talking about?"

Mike opens his eyes, but he doesn't turn to look up at you. From the side, the blue eye you can see seems to be glowing . . . or reflecting the blue of the bathroom tile. "Something," Mike repeats. "Yeah, I felt it. You didn't imagine it."

You slump a little, tension dropping out of your shoulders, which you hadn't known you were hunching. "Really?" you ask.

"Yeah," Mike says. He twists in your lap so the back of his head is against your leg, and those beautiful blue eyes are gazing directly up at your face.

He licks his lips. Does that mean he wants you to kiss him?

Oh, you'd love to kiss him . . . if he wasn't your best friend's boyfriend.

But when he was going to get sick, Sally laughed at him, didn't she? You're the one who helped him, you nursed him, while she stayed downstairs. She's probably flirting with Walt right now.

You gaze down at Mike, tenderly tracing the arch of his thick black eyebrows with your finger, while he looks up at you expectantly.

Don't even try to pretend that Sally won't be hurt — and furious — if you kiss Mike. Even if she's given him up, it would be too soon for you to jump in there, right?

But if she's really given him up, and truly doesn't care anymore, what's the harm?

You touch his upper lip with your fingertip, and that sensation makes you almost forget your own name.

Mike blinks at you.

He's waiting.

If you realize that you just can't do this to Sally and you say goodbye to Mike, turn to page 192. ➡

If you decide that now's totally the right time for your first kiss with Mike, turn to page 173. ➡

♥ You let out a deep breath and let yourself lean your full weight against Mike, enjoying his hug. You've got it really bad for him, so bad that you think you'd even pick him over Sally, if it came down to that.

Sally hasn't been all that great a friend to you lately anyway, always talking about herself, jabbering about her future modeling career. When's the last time she asked you a question about you? You and Sally talk about nothing but Sally.

You hold Mike — and you let him hold you — until you feel perfectly calm again. Then you step back and look up into his handsome face.

"I need to know something," you say softly. "Will you answer a question . . . a serious question?"

Mike shrugs. "Sure, why not," he replies.

"Okay," you say, "how do you really feel about Sally?"

You watch his face carefully for his reaction. Mostly he just looks thoughtful, and you're glad he's really taking your question seriously.

"I'm not sure how I feel about her," Mike says finally. "Really, I've only known her a little more than a week. I like her, I do. Now that I've met you, though . . . well, I really like you, too. I totally don't want to create a wedge between you two, but —"

You're struck with a brilliant idea. "I know!" you interrupt. *"Wedge!"* You pull out your plastic Frothmeister
gourmet coffee card and try to remember how doors get jim-
mied open on TV. Will this damage your Frothmeister card?
Oh, well, if you destroy it, the most you'll lose is a free chai
latte.

After taking a deep breath, you jam the card down between
the door frame and the door, sliding it under the latch.

The door swings open. You heave a big sigh of relief.

"Hey, how'd you do that?" Mike asks.

"I've got a few tricks up my sleeve," you reply.

"I'm sorry I'm not being more definite about your question," Mike says. "I wish I had a quick answer, but I don't."

You step through the doorway.

*If you tell Mike that it's okay, you can just let your
relationship ride and see what happens between him
and Sally with no pressure, turn to page 221.* ➡

*If you've had enough of his wishy-washiness and
insist that he give you a final answer about who
he's going to keep seeing, you or Sally, turn to
page 197.* ➡

Maybe it's seeing Mike so vulnerable after his arrogant attitude when you met him, but seeing him hugging the toilet, well . . . something in you just softens, and you take a step closer.

First you flush the existing evidence. Then you kneel down behind him and rub his back, softly soothing his muscle spasms.

He has a very nice back.

Who thought it was a good idea to put tiles decorated with drawings of exotic fish, along with their Latin names, randomly among the other plain blue tiles on the bathroom wall? Probably Darren's mother, duh. Drawings of fish is not the direction you would have gone in.

Mike hunches up his shoulders again and spews out another blast of hot glop. The deep, desperate breaths he takes after that almost make it sound like he's sobbing. You keep your hand still on his back, closing your eyes to ward off the smell. When he settles down, you flush again, and then you continue rubbing.

"I'm sorry," he whimpers. "It's awful."

"You'll think about what you're drinking next time, huh," you say.

"Yeah," he gasps. "If I live through this." He chuckles,

which makes him retch twice, shooting blanks both times. "Don't make me laugh," he moans.

"I think you're empty," you say. "Let me get you a glass of water, to clear the taste." You rinse out a cup somebody left in the bathroom earlier and give him some water. "Don't down it," you warn, "or it'll just come up again."

Mike sips carefully, and his stomach seems to have settled. "That was so horrible," he says. "The taste. Uk." He sits up and grabs a big bottle of blue mouthwash off the toilet tank. He swishes around and then spits out three different mouthfuls of that minty stuff before he's satisfied that the terrible flavor is gone.

"Oh, man," Mike says. "I'm wiped out." He leans back against you, and you sit back on the floor. He shifts around until he's resting his head in your lap, his face turned into your leg. You can feel his breath through the fabric of your jeans. "Thank you for helping me," he says quietly. "You didn't have to do that."

You can tell Mike's not a guy who says thank you a lot, so this actually means something coming from him.

He closes his eyes and tries to breathe steadily, curling up his body on the fuzzy blue mat. He tucks his hands around your knee, holding it.

While his eyes are closed, you gaze down at him. He looks the same as the guy you met on the field this afternoon, with the same smooth, tan skin on his cheek and neck, the bluish hint of beard on his chin, and the pretty, fleshy lips, but he seems so different to you now. There's no sign of the conceited teenage soccer jock who likes to boss people around. Now there's just a tired little boy who just threw up.

You're so touched that he's showing you this part of himself.

"Stroke my hair," Mike orders you in a whisper. "Gently."

You let out a quiet laugh. Well, his bossiness didn't change!

But right now you're finding even that cute.

If you realize that taking care of Mike proved you have real feelings for him and you admit that to him, turn to page 200. ➤

If you let yourself get overwhelmed with emotion and lean down to kiss his pretty lips, turn to page 173. ➤

If you realize that Mike's breath is still horrible even after the mouthwash and this makes you want to ditch him right there in the bathroom, no matter how cute he is, turn to page 179. ➤

"I have a date with Mike," you say, squaring your shoulders and trying to look more confident than you feel.

Shocked silence greets your announcement.

"Is this true?" Sally demands. She hits Mike on the shoulder. "Is this true?"

"No," he insists. "How could it be? I'm here with you."

"Then why is she saying that?" Sally demands. Her voice is rising to scary, shrill levels. When Mike shrugs, she wheels around to glare at you. "Why are you saying that?"

"Because it's true," you say flatly. You're stunned by Mike's denial that you had a date — you can barely process his response, it's so out of the range of what you ever considered possibly coming out of his mouth. "Mike, tell her the truth! You said the truth is always important. That's what you said!"

"I am telling the truth," he says. "Sally, why would I invite you both here at the same time? I think your friend is deeply confused . . . and really pathetic, if you ask me."

Totally involuntarily, you make a gagging sound in the back of your throat. This is going from bad to worse to insanely awful really quickly. A group of people you know from school starts to gather around where you're standing, excited to witness your humiliation.

"Why would you lie?" Sally yells at you. "That's so not like you —" She stops ranting, and her mouth drops open. "You're in love with him, aren't you? I can totally see it in your eyes!"

"No — he's in love with me!"

"You wish," Mike says.

It would have felt better if he'd punched you in the stomach.

"Not if you wished for a million years," Sally tells you. "Not if a fairy godmother used a magic spell to help you out — you still couldn't get Mike."

"He kissed me!" you wail.

"Ew, no way," says Mike. He shudders, and all his friends laugh.

You've got to get out of there with some dignity left — although it looks like you're going to be leaving without a boyfriend . . . or a best friend.

You try to keep your head up high as you walk out of the bowling alley, but Sally and Mike's laughter rings in your ears, and you can't help bursting into tears just as you make it outside into the parking lot alone.

There goes your happy ending. Next time, you're going to make some very different choices.

The End.

As you sit on the sand with your back against the log, resting your shoulder against Mike's athletic frame, suddenly everything clicks into place. You and Mike stare up at the twinkling stars, feeling like the only two people on Earth.

"I've got a silly question," Mike says. "What did you first think of me when you met me?"

You laugh, and snuggle closer to him. "That's not a silly question," you say. "That's a *dangerous* question."

"I'd like to know," Mike says.

You shift your position so you're almost curled up in Mike's lap, with your cheek against his chest. "I thought you were adorable," you tell him softly. "That's what I told Sally. But I didn't tell her that I . . . fell for you the moment I saw the beautiful electric blue of your eyes."

"My eyes, huh?" Mike asks with an amused snort. "Not my perfect biceps or my startling wit . . . or my amazing soccer skills?"

You laugh. "Or your total lack of modesty?" you joke, but then you turn serious again. "All those are very nice, too."

"Thank you," Mike says demurely, and you laugh again.

"Now my turn," you say. "Tell me what you first thought of me."

"Not much, really," Mike replies, and you hit him on the arm. "Ow! Well, it's true. If I thought anything, I was probably annoyed at your brother for kicking my butt on the field, and so I included you in that."

"How about later?" you ask.

"It changed not very long after," he says, "when you started telling me about your photo. And then . . . when I left you in the parking lot, when I left with Sally, I realized I was leaving with the wrong girl. I wanted to follow you. And that's why I came back."

You throw your arms around Mike and give him a giant hug. "Nobody has ever said anything that sweet to me. You're a big softie inside, aren't you, Michael?"

Mike grins down at you. "Now you know my deep, dark secret."

"I want to know all your secrets," you say, "and I'll keep all of them safe."

"I know you will," Mike says. "And that's why I want to be with you. There never really was any contest between you and Sally. Of course I choose you."

His words make you melt inside like chocolate.

Mike picks you up and turns your face toward his. Then he kisses you gently on the lips, soft pecks that tingle all the way down to your feet. It's not long before you're lost in the emotional connection that you've shared with Mike from the moment you looked into his eyes.

In the middle of one long kiss, you spare a moment to

think of Sally, surprised to find that the feeling of completeness you have with Mike totally overwhelms any guilt that you might have felt about stealing her boyfriend.

You didn't really *steal* Mike. Nobody can steal someone away from someone else unless the stolen person is willing to make the switch.

Yeah, you may lose Sally's friendship over this.

But that's just too bad for her. After all, all's fair in love and war.

Isn't it?

The End.

"That sounds like fun," you say. "Say hi to the dogs for me."

"What are you going to do?" Mike asks.

You pick up a folder of black-and-white 35mm film negatives from the desk beside you and show it to him. "I took some pictures of a river in the state park near my house — these are the negatives I already developed. I was planning on printing them in the darkroom. There's this student art show coming up really soon, so . . . I've got to stay here and get that done." You blush a little. "I was picked from the whole school to show my pictures, and the reception's going to be at city hall. It's kind of important to me."

"Wow. Can I watch you print the pictures?" asks Mike. "I've never seen real film being printed before."

Yes, you think, realizing that his interest in you just makes you want to tell him everything about your whole life. "I don't know," you say. You already feel totally comfortable with him — it would be great to have him hang out longer. A lot longer. But . . .

"C'mon, let me stay," Mike says. "I've got nothing but free time for a couple of hours. I can walk the dogs later . . . before I pick up Sally."

You think about what's in the negatives, exactly, that

Mike would see. Besides the nature photos, there are also a couple of pictures of Sally that you took for the modeling portfolio she's making for herself. Is that good or bad if Mike sees those? For a split second, you selfishly don't want him to be reminded of Sally at all. . . . But what are you *thinking*? It's good that Sally is on this roll — it will be like she's right in the darkroom with you and Mike, making sure you don't do anything stupid you'll regret.

"Yeah, okay," you tell him.

"Great," he says. A giant smile lights up his face. *Wow*, he's cute when he smiles. It makes you feel a little woozy, but you tell yourself that the smile didn't really mean anything. He mentioned his date with Sally a second ago, so it's obvious that he just thinks of you as a friend. Not even his friend, really — his girlfriend's friend. It should be safe to have him hang around.

As you get to work setting up the darkroom, Mike sits on a stool and watches quietly. You fill up three trays with developer, stop bath, and fixing fluid, turn on the red safelight, and expose the first of your negatives onto photo paper through an enlarger. You call him over when the photo is surfacing on the paper in the developer tray.

"That's amazing," Mike whispers, as a picture of the river comes clear.

You slide the photo into the stop bath for fifteen seconds, and stare at it while it's sitting in the fixer for two minutes. It's an okay shot of the river, you decide — pretty, showing the sunlight through the trees, the dappled forest floor, the water rushing downstream in foamy twists between the shiny rocks. But you hope there are better shots to come, maybe ones where the glare off the rocks won't look so harsh in black and white.

"You're good at this," Mike points out. "You like it a lot, I can tell."

"I love photography," you reply. "It's . . . it's like a mixture of magic and science. I know it's the right combination of chemicals and light that makes a picture develop, but when the image appears suddenly on the white paper, it still feels like magic every time."

"Print another one," Mike urges.

You decide to get it over with and print a picture of Sally. She's sitting in a porch swing, looking very happy. She's laughing and looks beautiful, the sunlight hitting her translucent hair and lighting it up like a halo around her head.

"Wow," Mike says. "That's awesome. She looks old-fashioned and totally *now* at the same time."

From his reaction, it's completely clear to you that he's deeply in love with Sally. "You know," you say, "I think it's really cool that you started seeing Sally — you guys seem great together. Happy. A cute couple."

"Yeah," Mike says, in a tone you totally cannot decipher. "Thanks." Was that *thanks* a little bit sarcastic?

"We've been friends forever," you continue, even though you feel like you're babbling now, "and I love her to death.

Sally's like a sister to me." With a pair of tongs, you pull Sally's photo out of the fixer tray, and cross the room to clip the picture onto a clothesline so it can air dry.

Mike follows you, and you both stand there looking at the dangling photo for a second.

"Doesn't she look beautiful?" you ask.

"Yeah, Sally's beautiful," Mike says. He shrugs. "She's great, but she doesn't . . . she can't . . ."

"What?"

"Tell me if this makes sense," Mike says. "I was thinking about this in the shower this morning. Sally's talent is herself — the way she looks, the way she acts . . . she can radiate just like she's doing in this picture."

"That makes total sense," you say. "I've seen her glow a lot of times. She can just kind of turn it on."

"But it's all surface," Mike continues. "You know what I mean?"

Suddenly you feel defensive. Is he insulting your best friend? "There's more to her than just being beautiful."

"Not like you," he says.

"Excuse me?" Did he just insult *you* now?

"No, no, don't take that the wrong way," he says quickly. "Sally can radiate beauty, but you have the talent to capture it as art . . . and to me, that's a lot more interesting. Her art is her outside, while yours is inside. Does that sound crazy?"

"No," you say, but you can't help wondering if he just

told you how much prettier Sally is than you are. "She's definitely beautiful, though . . ."

Mike stiffens next to you, then reaches out to tap the corner of Sally's photo with a finger. It wobbles in the air. "So are you," he says.

You feel a strong yearning toward him and you lean forward. His lips are so close to yours.

If you lunge forward and kiss him, turn to page 36. ➡

If you think that it's too soon for a kiss, that it would make things weird between you and Sally, and that you should leave the darkroom right now, turn to page 199. ➡

"Uh . . ." you say. You've got nothing.

"Well?" Sally demands. She's starting to sound hurt.

Desperately, you reach into your pockets for some inspiration — anything! — and your hand closes around the coupon for a free game.

Suddenly you know what to say.

"Remember my horrible Aunt Hortense?" you ask Sally. She nods.

"Well, she's visiting this week," you breezily lie, "and she's showing slides of her cruise through the Alaskan icebergs, so you know I just wanted to be anywhere but there. I finished my paper earlier than I thought, so when I found this coupon for a free game of bowling —" You pull the coupon out of your pocket and show it to Sally.

She snatches it out of your hand and reads it quickly.

"I thought I'd head over here and practice my game," you finish. "I called to see if you wanted to come with me, but I guess you'd already left."

Sally hands back your coupon. "Sorry," she says. "I had my cell off for a little while. It was just so surprising and weird that you were here."

"Just coincidence!" you chirp.

"Hey," Mike says, "should we all play together? Then we can all bowl for free if we use your coupon."

Sally doesn't seem thrilled with that suggestion — she clearly wants this time with Mike to herself — but how can she argue with a free game?

She can't. At least not without seeming jealous.

Which she is. This is one of the reasons you're getting a little sick of hanging around Sally all the time. Her attitude is really getting on your nerves. She's so cold-blooded about cutting you out of her life when there's a guy around that she likes.

The three of you bowl for a while, and although Mike's a really good bowler, you try to keep your praise for him to a minimum. Still, you can't help cheering and hugging him when he makes three strikes in a row.

Sally narrows her eyes at you. "I'll be right back," she says. "Bathroom break."

The second Sally's safely out of earshot, Mike gestures for you to come closer to him. "She overheard me telling a friend of mine that I was thinking of going bowling," he explains in a whisper, "so I had to invite her along."

"I thought you were going to break up with her," you hiss at him.

"I couldn't," he replies. "It's going to hurt her. I've got to wait for the right time."

"No time like the present," you say, hoping it would sound like a joke. It doesn't.

Mike shakes his head. "Not yet," he says. "But I'll make it up to you. How about if I take you out on a proper date tomorrow night?" He smiles warmly at you.

At the sight of his smile, your knees go weak and you have trouble remembering how annoying it is that your bowling date got ruined. "That will work," you say. You pick up your bowling ball and march up to the line just as Sally returns from the bathroom.

You heave the bowling ball and knock down all the pins but two, then easily pick up the spare.

As far as you're concerned, tomorrow night can't arrive fast enough.

If you're ready for your big date, turn to page 228. ➡

Now that you've let Mike off the hook and told him that he doesn't need to make a decision right away, he noticeably relaxes around you. You smile to yourself, glad you didn't pressure him into choosing between you and Sally before he was sure who he wanted.

Your task is to make him want you.

"So, thanks to your brilliant use of a coffee card, we escaped," Mike says. "Good timing, too, because I've got to get going —"

Mike's cellphone rings. He checks the caller ID. "Sally," he tells you, and then flips his phone open. "Hey, Sal," he answers. "What's up?"

You scan his face as he listens, but you can't make out what he thinks about what Sally's saying.

"Okay," he tells her. "It's not a problem. No, really, it's cool. We'll . . . just reschedule. Yeah. Talk to you later." Mike clicks the phone closed.

"What?" you ask. "Is she okay?"

"She's fine," Mike replies. "Her grandmother stopped by unexpectedly, and they're all going out to dinner or something. She's pretty annoyed."

"I'm sure she's fuming," you say. You pull out your own cellphone and turn off the ringer before Sally can call and tell you all about how angry she is to be missing her date. It's amazing how little guilt you feel over this. You know that it's rotten of you to be so happy that Sally had to cancel . . . but you're too gleeful to really give it much thought right now.

"So now I'm free tonight," Mike tells you. "What should we do now?"

"I'm up for anything," you reply. "Any suggestions?"

"The air in that tiny room was stale and gross," Mike says. "I'd really like to breathe fresh air. Want to take a walk down the beach?"

"Absolutely," you say. "I'll take walking along an endless horizon over being trapped in a teeny space every single time."

As the sun gets lower in the sky, Mike drives you to the shore and parks in an empty lot. You both leave your shoes in the car, so you have to step gingerly over the pebbly part where the beach meets the road before you get to the soft, cool sand beyond.

You and Mike walk down the beach, leaving footprints at the water's edge, giggling as you step over beached jellyfish. The water is roaring in your ears, and the setting sun turns all the sand a lovely shade of pink. You can't remember the last time you felt this easy and happy. The feeling makes you want to ask Mike something personal about his life.

"Do you have any brothers or sisters?" you ask him.

He gives you a funny look. "Why?"

"No reason," you say quickly, alarmed at his change of mood. "I was just curious."

"C'mon, let's go sit down," Mike says, pointing to a bleached log that has washed ashore.

After you get comfortable sitting next to Mike on the sand with your back against the log, he clasps his hands in his lap and stares up at the sky.

"I have a little brother," he says, "but he doesn't live with us."

"How old is he?" you ask.

"Eight?" Mike wonders out loud. "Yeah, he hasn't turned nine yet."

You swallow. "Why doesn't he live with you?"

"Okay, I'm getting to that," Mike says. "I haven't even told Sally this yet." He pauses, and you wait patiently until he's ready to keep talking. "Okay, well, when Robby was a baby, a light bulb exploded right next to his crib. Just a freak thing — light bulbs explode sometimes. Not often, but sometimes. Anyway, the explosion blinded him, permanently."

You reach out and grab one of Mike's hands. He takes your hand and holds it in both of his.

"So he goes to a school on the other side of the state," Mike continues. "He lives there year-round, so I don't get to hang out with him much. It's a great school, and he's a good, happy kid, really. But I wish I could spend more time with him."

You lean your head against Mike's shoulder and stare out at the setting sun, feeling the warmth of his hand around yours. "I'm glad you told me," you say. "I hope I get to meet Robby someday."

The colors shift in the sky, and the clouds turn yellow and pink, then dark like bruises, before the sun drops over the horizon and darkness falls.

"It's getting late," you say. "My curfew on a school night is really harsh."

Mike squeezes your hand. "Stay a little longer," he says. "Stay longer and I'll drive you home when we're both ready to go."

You sigh, wondering what to do. Your father is insanely strict about curfew, and you know that each second that you're late is another second that he wonders if he should call the police to find you. Curfew is really your father's only unreasonable rule.

Mike still hasn't made a decision between you and Sally, you remind yourself. Why should you break your father's most important rule for someone who ultimately may choose your best friend over you?

Still, if you do stay out later with Mike, you might get the chance to show him once and for all that you're the right girl for him.

If you stay with Mike on the beach longer, turn to 210. ➡

If you ask him to take you home right then, and tell him that he needs to choose you over Sally before you'll break family rules for him, turn to page 197. ➡

Before you can talk yourself out of it, you tip the cup up and take a big swallow of the mixture.

The guys and Sally make the expected and appropriate grossed-out noises.

Quickly, before the flavor can hit you, you take another swig and gulp that, too. There's still way too much left in the cup.

Yuck — coffee and cola don't mix well at all. The flavors combine to taste like an old charcoal briquette.

Next to you, Mike gags suddenly and spits out the foul brew into the sink. "Uck," he says, spitting to clear his mouth.

Then the pickle juice kicks in under the burst taste of coffee ashes. Oh, no. Your brain processes this flavor as a hundred different kinds of wrong. It tastes like cold death, and you have the sudden sensation that your stomach is dropping while you're having a total head rush.

"She's turning green!" Walt cheers.

Now you make your worst mistake — *you take another sip of the potion.*

That's when the curdled half-and-half hits your intestines. *No*, your pipes say, in very audible gurgling. *Uh-uh.*

"Are you okay?" Sally asks, sounding worried.

"Fine," you gasp. "I just need some air. Air."

"She's going to blow chunks," Spencer notes.

That disgusting phrase reminds you of the curdled cream chunks you swallowed.

Your internal system will not accept this kind of treatment.

You can't barf at a party. You just can't. That is in no way something you will feel good about doing.

Especially not with Mike and the guys watching.

With a sickening flash, you remember you had sweet and sour chicken for dinner. It was bright orange, and so sweet it tasted like candy.

You clap a hand over your mouth, gag horribly once, and then bolt for the kitchen back door. It leads to a wide, slightly overgrown lawn with a bright spotlight shining onto the grass. The screen door slams behind you as you stumble into the yard, looking for a place to let go.

"There she is!" Mike shouts.

"Go!" says somebody else.

There's got to be bushes somewhere. You can't barf in the spotlight! You stumble back toward the house, trying not to breathe.

Turn to page 188. ➡️

♥ Right on time, Mike picks you up for your dinner date. He even brings you a flower (just a carnation, but still) and compliments you on your new dress (which is a skirt, but still). As he drives you toward the beach, where he's made a reservation at a swanky restaurant overlooking the ocean, you just know this is going to be one of the most romantic nights of your life.

At the restaurant, surrounded by all the sophisticated couples, you suddenly feel like a little girl playing dress-up, pretending to be an adult. You squirm awkwardly in your seat, completely at a loss for something to say to Mike, while trying to pay attention to the menu at the same time. It's all fish dishes, and you can barely remember what each fish is like enough to choose.

Finally, you decide on something that sounds simple, and you glance up at Mike. He's shifting around nervously in his seat, staring around the room like he thinks every-body's watching him.

"What are you getting?" you ask him.

"Uh, I haven't decided yet," he says. "I've barely looked. Hey, is this weird for you at all? Being in here on a date with all these grownups?"

"Yeah, totally," you tell him warmly, so pleased that he's feeling the same thing you are. "I decided not to worry about it, though. If anyone is looking at us at all, they're probably thinking what a cute young couple we are."

"You think?"

"Absolutely."

After that, you both relax and enjoy the meal, which is wonderfully sumptuous. You chat easily with Mike about school stuff mostly, safe topics, but with every word you say to him you try to get across how much you like him.

After Mike pays the check, you smile and thank him. The dinner date could not have gone better . . . it was entirely glamorous.

"Do you want to take a walk on the beach?" Mike asks. "Burn off some of those calories in that insane dessert?"

"Sure," you say, and he follows you out of the restaurant and across a short boardwalk.

At the wooden stairs leading down to the sand, you stop. "I'm not sure I'm dressed for the beach," you say.

"C'mon," he says. "You won't ruin your dress. Just take off your shoes. I'll even hold them for you."

How can you say no to that offer?

But something has changed with Mike now that the sun is beginning to set — he starts getting melancholy.

"Sally would have loved that dessert," he says. "Dark chocolate like that is her favorite."

"Huh," you say. It's not like Sally has the world rights to dark chocolate. "I like it a lot, too. Maybe more than she does."

"Yeah, probably," Mike agrees halfheartedly.

You walk in silence along the shoreline for a few yards before Mike speaks again. "The other day when I was meeting Sally's parents —"

"I don't really want to talk about Sally," you interrupt. "I'm really enjoying being here with you, all alone with you."

Mike takes a deep breath. "Yeah," he says. "Sally told me that I harp on one thought too many times. I've got to stop that."

If you try to totally change the mood, and bring Mike over to a nearby driftwood log where you can sit with him and talk about something else, turn to page 210. ➤

If you get insulted by how much he's talking about Sally, insist that he has to choose between you, and demand to be taken home immediately, turn to page 197. ➤

About the Author

J. E. Bright is the author of a bunch of novels, novelizations, and novelty books for children and young adults. He lives in Soho, New York, with a good, fat cat named Gladys, and an evil, skinny cat named Mabel. He wishes he had more decision-making opportunities in his own romantic life.

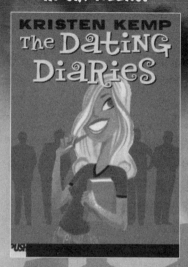